The Adventures of
Micah Mushmelon,
Boy Talmudist

The Adventures of Micah Mushmelon, Boy Talmudist

A comic strip epic in prose

by

Michael Wex

QUATTRO BOOKS

Cover cartoon illustration of Micah Mushmelon
Copyright © 2007 by Graham Robson.

Cover Design and Typography: Julie McNeill, McNeill Design Arts

Library and Archives Canada Cataloguing in Publication

Wex, Michael
        The adventures of Micah Mushmelon, boy Talmudist :
a comic strip epic in prose / Michael Wex.

ISBN 978-0-9782806-2-8

        I. Title.

PS8595.E93A74 2007   C813'.54
C2007-904489-1

Published by
Quattro Books
P.O. Box 53031
Royal Orchard Postal Station
10 Royal Orchard Blvd.
Thornhill, ON L3T 3C0
www.quattrobooks.ca

Printed in Canada

A glossary of Yiddish and Hebrew terms will be found at the end of the book.

I

"HATE THE GOYIM AS YOU MIGHT, Potasznik, it cannot be denied." Micah Mushmelon, Boy Talmudist, slammed his fist onto the table, leaned forward and stuffed his mouth with chickpeas. I waited expectantly. What apparent paradox, what seeming contradiction of all the rules of empirical observation was about to come out of him now?

I took a long look at the boy in the chair opposite. He was possessed of a cone-shaped, somewhat foreshortened body, softish and plumpish, tapering downwards and slightly out of true to a pair of tiny flat feet that could still have borne baby-shoes—a punching bag with fringes in the middle. A *kashkèt*, called by him a *dashikl*, rested on the top of his head; this was a bloated satin Dutch-boy cap affected by hasidic children of Polish descent, beneath which, in the case of this child, lay a blotched, cantaloupian face, a ten-cent sack of freckle misshapes, a coconut-flecked, kosher-for-Passover marshmallow with a mouth. "Were I to reveal myself as I am," he would say with a meaningful stretch upwards, "could Schwarzenegger support his family? Would anyone publish Susan Sontag? *Someone* has to keep the world in balance."

How wobbly young Mushmelon had been made aware of his calling—while herding his sheep in Prospect Park or sitting alone in an empty *bes-medresh*, flicking the lights on the memorial plaques and waiting for a sign—no one ever knew, and Micah himself was understandably loath to tell. But that he had been chosen to re-align the world—to this I can attest from my own experience.

Not three days prior to the time of which I write, I was a failure, a nothing. Life stretched before me as vast and empty as a Torah scroll from which all the letters have fled. An eleven year old pariah, I had been cashiered from Oykrei Horim, the Mountain Uprooters, a crack troop of mitsve commandos, on false charges brought by suborned witnesses. "He eats kasha with buttermilk," they claimed. "He goes to the dentist on Passover and his mother is a racial Litvak." Who said it's easy to be a Jew? The insignium was ripped from my cap, the edges torn from my official Oykrei Horim fringed undergarment, and I was pronounced dead. Rabbi Lester Dean, the company commander, led the troop in Kaddish. They even threw handfuls of dirt on me.

My weeks of exile gave me a new appreciation of the history and travails of my unfortunate people. I was solitary as a stone, with only the wind to talk to. I devoted my life to comic books, trading cards, crossword puzzles—the aliments of youth outcast. And then, two days after Yom Kippur in the year nineteen-dash-*epes*, I cast my eye upon the little child who was to lead me—into life and adventure, into Torah, spousehood and good deeds.

The truth is, he cast his eye upon me. I was rushing out of Kosher Komix and Kurios with my final three packages of *Arzei Levonoyn*, The Torah Giants Trading Card Game—if I had no one with whom to trade, I'd *buy* the whole set myself—and with my nose buried inside the latest issue of my favourite Yiddish language comic book, *Khamoro Kadisho, The Holy Donkey*, subtitled

Di vinderlikhe nesies fun Plapelisa, dem heyliken tannas Rebbin Pinkhas ben Yoirs ayzele, ayn khumoyr kudoysh ve-noyeym, which is to say, *The Marvellous Journeys of Plapelisa, the Donkey of the Holy Tanna Rabbi Pinkhas ben Yair, a Holy Donkey Who Could Speak.* Nothing else mattered: Balaam's ass and Absalom's head could kiss me where the Jews reposed. They *had* to have printed my letter: I had grown-ups cross me over busy streets, and never made skips in my prayers. My fingers were trembling like fish at the Judgment—I could be a published commentator and not even know it, a Rashi of my own little world—when my elbow caught the face of a dwarfish figure waddling in the opposite direction.

After I'd hauled it up from the sidewalk, it looked me up and down, re-adjusted its skewed *dashikl* and casually spat out a front tooth. *"Ve-ki yigakh shoyr,"* it snarled, "If an ox gores a man, it should give him at least a piece kleenex to staunch the bleeding. You know, of course, that it's *osur*, forbidden, to swallow your own bleeding blood."

I reached in my pocket and gave him. "That's better," he hummed through a mouthful of tissue. "Now they can't give me braces."

He poked me appraisingly, like a cannibal with qualms about *kashrus*, and took a look at my comic. "Mmh." He snorted in Yiddish. "When I was a child, I thought like a child; when I became a man I gave up childish ways, and so should you. And don't ever read what I'm quoting." He stuck out his hand. I shook it in return. *"Nu?"*

"Potasznik. Shraga Potasznik."

"And I am Micah Mushmelon, Boy Talmudist."

The name meant nothing to me.

"And you, Potasznik, you must be a gossip columnist, you're so *gleikhgiltik* when it comes to celebrities."

I had no idea he was famous. To me, he was just another overweight nine year old, one of thousands to be found in our neighbourhood, only his *payes* hung down to his waist.

"You're looking at my *payes*, I see. Don't have time to cut 'em. As for the rest of my hair, it's been so long since I've removed my trusty *dashikl* here"—he tapped the crown and I heard a hollow sound—"that it's all fallen out due to lack of sunlight and air. I wanted to solve the problem before I had to start putting on *tefillin* ... But I see you still don't know who I am, do you?

I had to confess to the truth.

"Eyes but they see not, ears but they hear not. You've heard of the recent kosher candy scandal?"

I had indeed. I had been deprived of everything, that worst summer of my life: Two Tablets of the Jaw, every kid's favourite giant-sized sour-cherry strictly kosher sucky pill, sold only in the unbreakable duo-pack, was revealed to contain pigs'-foot jelly. The news justified the Name of Heaven, and explained the traffic fatalities visited upon so many religious children in the recent past—even the Hungarians used to eat it. More frightening still, the management of the firm had been exonerated: one of their trusted *kashrus* inspectors had been spiking the ingredients of his own accord, not even taking a pay-off, simply to bring Jewish children into the hands of transgression. The inspector had vanished; all the investigators knew was that his name was phoney, his Social Security number that of a deceased Catholic priest, may God protect us.

Did I remember the kosher candy scandal? I was a two pack a day man, how could I forget it? I spent three days crouched over the toilet, beating my breast between spasms.

"Well," Mushmelon went on, "If you remember it—and judging from the number of fillings in your mouth, you must—you'll be glad to know that it was I who uncovered it. I, Micah Mushmelon, Boy Talmudist, with the help of the heavenly technique of *shakle ve-tarye*, dialectic toss-and-catch, I solved it"—he was jumping up and down, the kleenex hanging out of his mouth, and people were starting to stare—"even if I failed to apprehend the perpetrator." He removed the kleenex from his mouth, studied it and then set it afire right on the sidewalk with a lighter he'd pulled from his pocket. "And now, Potasznik, now that you have some hint of with whom you have to do—and I assure you, it's only a hint—tell me, which way are you going? Perhaps you'd like to repair to my digs for a *minkhe* and a Mayim Khayim."

Mushmelon's "digs," as he called his residence, turned out to be the entire second floor of the synagogue and yeshiva of the hasidim of Hipst, an older building from which the Woolworth sign had never been removed—"It still brings 'em in," he said—and in which Micah lived by himself. He had a staff, but no parents. "There are evil forces about," was all he would tell them about them. For the rest, he informed me that he was the grandson of the old Hipster Rebbe, and, as such, was in fact the current Hipster Rebbe himself. The hasidim were simply waiting for him to attain his majority before entrusting their lives to him.

"I do as I please," he told me.

"But where do you go to school? The Hipster yeshiva is for grown-ups."

He looked at me with disdain. "*Se zol mayn fis mir vern a rebbe?* My foot, my tutor? I was finished school before you ever started. It is said that the Gaon of Vilna was lecturing to adults by the time he was six; at six I had published my first volume of responsa, *Mikha Moykha*." The implication that rabbis had been sending him legal questions since he was about two years old was not lost on me. Nor was the "first."

"But what about the government?" I asked incredulously. "Even if you've been through yeshiva, what about English? I mean, there's a law. You can't quit school until you're sixteen."

"But you can finish it anytime." He pointed towards the wall. "My senior matric," he said proudly. "Too bad the prom was on a Friday night." I looked at the date; he would have been nine months old.

He went on to tell me of his low community-profile, of the crime-fighting work which accounted for this secretiveness; he gave me a reading list and offered to do all my homework. "I need an assistant, a companion, a helpmeet and a playmate. I'll have a letter sent to your parents offering you a scholarship to the *Talmud Torah vi-Yeshiva de-Khasidei Hipst be-Amerike.* That should give you enough free time."

"But there's no such thing," I protested.

"Where there's a letterhead, Potasznik, there must be an entity. And if you were better educated, you'd realize that I've just solved the nominalist-realist controversy that's bedeviled western philosophy for nigh on a thousand years." He reached for an old-fashioned bell-pull and gave it a tug. A moment later a servant appeared, clad in hasidic-style livery. Micah made the introductions. "Shraga-Getsl, Potasznik; Potasznik, Shraga-Getsl." We nodded to each other. "Shraga-Getsl was head of a yeshiva in Europe until he came under my grandfather's influence, weren't you, Shraga-Getsl?"

"The rebbe is correct as usual," replied Shraga-Getsl, beaming.

"Yes. Potasznik will be working with us. Get out the Talmud Torah letterhead and send his parents an offer of free tuition. Tell them we've had our eye on him for a while. Outline a curriculum for them—and don't think you won't be following it, Potsy—send it by courier and follow up with a phone-call. And don't forget to use your full title … Where your folks from, Potasznik?"

"They were born here, but my grandparents came from Plotsk."

"Better and better. Shraga-Getsl—your middle name isn't Getsl by any chance, is it?"

"No, it's Faivel."

"Faivel getsl ten," he said. Shraga-Getsl collapsed with laughter. "Enough!" Micah cried. "Shraga-Getsl was rabbi in Biala for a while. They'll like that. Go with Shraga-Getsl and give him your address."

I stood dumbfounded in the office. "Is it all true what he says, Reb Shraga-Getsl?"

"You ain't heard the half of it. He makes the *yanuka*, the sacred suckling of the Zohar, look like Sabu the Elephant Boy."

"Who's that?"

"Never mind. Forget you ever heard it. Pretend I said Lou Costello."

I was getting lost. Shraga-Getsl was as obscure as Mushmelon was brilliant.

"There's something I don't understand, Reb Shraga-Getsl."

"*Nu?*"

"If Micah Mushmelon's work is so important, if it's so involved that even a wild genius like him needs an assistant …"

"Yeah?"

"Well, why me? I mean, we only just met a couple of hours ago, and already he's ready to trust me with such important stuff?"

Shraga-Getsl laughed. "You think it's an accident that *you* banged into *him* outside the comic book store this afternoon?" He seemed to be stressing the wrong words. "You think it's an accident I should know this when neither of you has had a chance to tell me? We've been looking for you, Potasznik, searching and waiting, making sure."

"Making sure of what?"

Shraga-Getsl tapped the side of his lengthy nose with an index finger.

"Micah's gonna tell me?"

"*Azoy.* Just like the messiah, in his own good time."

"But you still haven't told me, why me?"

"Why? Beside your noble character? You really want to know?" I'd have given two month's allowance. "Your name is Shraga and you were thrown out of Oykrei Horim."

Which was like telling me, because I was born. I could see where Oykrei Horim might have had something to do with things, but my name? "Your name's Shraga, too."

"No. My name's Shraga-Getsl. Do you ever use your middle name?"

"Are you kidding? You think I'm ninety years old?"

"I'm surprised you're even eleven. Don't you see? We were looking for a real Shraga, a naked Shraga, so to speak."

I had no intention of taking off my clothes for anybody, and I told him so. He threw up his arms and sent me home.

HE WAS A MUSHMELON on his father's side only. His mother had been a Dovshinsky, the daughter and only child of Rabbi Yoysef Yerakhmiel Dovshinsky, Grand Rabbi of the Holy Congregation of Hipst.

Over the course of the next day and a half, what with my own urgent interest and the suddenly loosened tongues of my parents—it isn't every day that every boy is offered a scholarship out of the blue, and when that boy has been a social leper, a Georgy-Porgy, a *shmuck*, a *shmendrik*, a *shmegege*, a hobbledehoy addicted to crossword puzzles and comic books for all his eleven years (so much so that his parents, whom he could overhear at night, would happily have sacrificed ten or even twenty percent of his astoundingly high school average for just a drop, a dollop of normal childikkayt, be it even *botl bi-shishim*, voided sixty times over by his remaining quirks)—when said boy is not exactly your Jew next-door's Berele ben Shmerele from Blutepolsk, the *simkhe*, the joy, in the house is like Purim and *Simkhes Toyre*, the Rejoicing in the Law, combined with New Year's Eve and Mardi Gras. My father phoned in my acceptance even before I was supposed to have known of the offer. He bought a bottle of slivovitz, and he and my mother toasted their brilliant son, the two parents *shepping nakhes*. They had no friends either. And as they drank, they spoke. Louder and louder, magnifying their praise of the holy Hipster dynasty. Between my parents' talk and my father's books on hasidic history—not to mention my mother's storybooks on the same subject, *Fantastic Wonder Tales in Yiddish*—I managed to get a bit of a picture of what I was getting into.

Yoysef Yerakhmiel Dovshinsky was born in 1885 in Stara Bielizna, the son of the Holy Water-Carrier, of blessed memory, a man who would assuredly have been one of the thirty-six hidden saints on account of whom God keeps the world alive, had he not been so generally accounted a member of that company. Reb Shimi-Yentes, as he was known, *shlepped* his pails with joy, serving the scholars of the *bes-medresh* for free. Every night, he would draw water by himself and mop the floor of the holy place, taking care never to be seen doing so.

One night he was caught by the local rabbi, David Israel Zemelbekker, famed under his initials as the Holy DIZ. Marvelling at the zest with which the water-carrier, surely exhausted by now after a full-day's physical labour, went about his self-appointed task, the DIZ made him a promise: *"Zol der oybershter gebn az di vest bald hobn a zin vus vet makhn mitn gantsn folk yisroel azoy vi di makhst mitn vashbezem*, May the Lord soon grant that you have a son who will swing the whole Jewish people the way you're swinging your mop."

From the mouth of the righteous to the ear of the Lord. Scarcely ten months later, Shimi and Yente held a bris for their first (and *nebekh*, only) son, who more than fulfilled the prophecy of the DIZ. As the official biography described it, he grew up to be "simple in his piety, wimpled in sobriety, yet so forceful in society that he started a revolution in Jewish life that has continued from his day into our own."

A prodigy, he uttered not a single profane word, no word not directed to prayer or learning, before his bar-mitzvah. After his marriage and appointment as rabbi in Hipst, hard by the River Waut, he found himself embroiled in a dispute with the local secularists. Hipst had long had an evil name as a centre of "enlightenment" and assimilation, and its last three rabbis, young men all, had died of heart failure within three years of their respective appointments. In Dovshinsky, however, the local Hellenizers had met more than their equal. Through a distant cousin on his mother's side, a Cantor Yoelson of Washington, D.C., Rabbi Yoysef Yerakhmiel had been receiving packages from America containing, among other interesting matter, cylinders, later '78 recordings, of some of the cantorial stars of the New World. Mixed into one package of these were a number of recordings by King Oliver, the Original Dixieland Jazz Band and Jelly Roll Morton. Dovshinsky, who could not at the time read the Latin alphabet, was amazed and enthused at what he took to be American innovations in traditional Jewish music, and, knowing no better, began to incorporate the melodies and musical principles learned from these records into the worship in his synagogue. As word of his innovations began to spread, as the line of snake-dancing pietists spilling out of the synagogue grew longer and more frenzied with each passing Sabbath (certain completist reference works on popular music and dance credit Rabbi Dovshinsky with the spontaneous re-invention and subsequent popularization of the conga-line), the town of Hipst experienced a religious revival unparalleled since the days of the Baal Shem Tov and his first disciples. Within the space of a few months, there was only a handful of assimilation-ists remaining in Hipst, all of whom eventually left the town.

Of course, the Rebbe had his opponents. The word came in from the Carpathians: "There is nothing new in the Torah." The Hipster responded with a pamphlet, *Ein Garin be-Ungarin*, proving that Hungary did not exist. The Rebbes in Poland objected strenuously to his new order of divine service until they discovered that the Lithuanian Rabbis had laid it under the ban. The Polish leaders then became his fervent defenders, even while forbidding their own followers to enter a Hipster *bes-medresh*.

But the Hipster's time had come. Crowds of jeering hasidim would surround Litvak yeshivas and chant, *"Shlog mikh, tate, akht mul tsum takt,"* for hours, until the Litvaks, *tsetumelt* and distrait, called in the non-Jewish police. They informed the authorities that Hipster hasidism was a front for the Polish Bolsheviks; the Hipster produced his autographed picture of Paderewski, signed, "To Joe from Iggy—keep swinging," and a number of prominent Litvaks spent the month in jail. The Hipster, to show that there were no hard feelings, arranged for and raised their bail himself.

Storm clouds were gathering over Europe, and the Hipster didn't want to get wet. After his first wife died in childbirth, he decided to leave Poland for the new world; when told that even the doorknobs in America were *treyf*, the Rebbe replied that he'd slaughter his himself.

He settled near Boise, Idaho. *"Ikh hob gevolt zayn noent tsum bulbe-tsenter,"* he later explained. "I wanted to be near the potato centre." After four years in New Hipst, Idaho, followed by the notorious Defeat of New Orleans, after which he ruled that fig mould was the equivalent of pork, the Rebbe finally moved to Brooklyn, where he established his *bes-medresh* and related institutions, all under the collective designation, Shoymer Pesoyim,

Protector of Idiots (see Psalm 116), an ironic allusion to his set-backs in the new world.

As tiny as it was devoted, the community of American Hipsters became something of a Brooklyn landmark. Like their contemporaries, the M'lochim, their small numbers belied their influence, even while leaving the Rebbe free to pursue his own work. He was the first person in rabbinic garb to become a regular on Fifty-Second Street, where he subsequently became known as the Chief Rabbi of Birdland. His strong anti-drug stance—*"Mir klekt a shmek,* snuff is enough"—coupled with the wisdom of a man of God, is credited with saving more than one jazz musician from debauchery and early death. So esteemed was he, that even non-Jewish musicians took to referring to themselves as Hipsters, in tribute to Rabbi Dovshinsky. Perhaps the greatest disappointment of his career was his failure to convert Charlie Parker. *"Ven der foygl volt zikh toyvl gevezn un geleygt yedn tug tefillin,"* he once sighed, "If Bird had but converted and laid *tefillin* every day, I could have got him nice, steady work in my choir."

The Rebbe was on his fourth wife by the time he finally had a child, a girl. *"Dus hot mir gefelt,"* he moaned on hearing the news, and he accordingly named the child Felle, eventually giving her in marriage to Rabbi Simkhe-Ber Mushmelon, grandson of one of the pioneer Hipsters who had accompanied the Rebbe from Poland to Idaho, and the first baby born in New Hipst II, after that upstate colony was established in the mid-fifties (an inter-dynastic marriage was impossible, as all other hasidic groups had long since banned intermarriage with the Hipsters). Two years after the birth of their son, Micah, and while Felle was pregnant with her second child, the young couple was found dead in their house in New Hipst II. Felle had been suffocated with her wig, while Simkhe-Ber had been bludgeoned to death with a blunt instrument, a hardback copy of *As a Driven Leaf*, a well-known novel by a Conservative Rabbi concerning the life and activities of the heretic, Elisha ben Avuyah, may the name of the wicked rot. There were no fingerprints on the book or anywhere else in the house, and the case was never solved.

Israel is not a widower, praise God. The child Micah was in New York visiting his grandfather at the time of the tragedy. The old sage had vowed not to leave the city until such time as the pork-merchant gangsters in Jerusalem ceased their relentless persecution of religious Jews and allowed construction of a new Hipster yeshiva on the site of the Knesset. "I'm not even asking they should throw it down," said the Rebbe, "all I want is the space."

Stricken though he was by the loss of his only child, the Father of Hipsters and Master of Strategic Reversals sought solace in the rearing and education of his grandson, in the molding of a new Hipster to take his place after a hundred and twenty years.

Yet the boy was odd, almost wilfully so. Tone deaf, with two left feet, he could barely tell "Candy Man" from *Kol Nidre*. He was fat and ungainly, couldn't even conga in time. Much as the old man hated to admit it, young Micah—for all his *yikhes*—had, by some whim of all-seeing Providence, been endowed with the brain of a Litvak. "And I think I knew the Litvak," his grandfather remarked cryptically. Where the Alter Hipster had been known to take up to sixty-four choruses of *Adoyn Oylom*, Micah would recite his prayers in a monotonous undertone better suited to a shopping list than praise of the Almighty. He was in too much of a hurry to get back to his books; there was usually one he hadn't yet read. With the exception of his grandfather, he had no respect for any recent rabbi whatever. Only Rabbi Rozin of Dvinsk, known as the Genius of Rogatchow, escaped his criticism, though Micah did consider him a little slow off the mark.

Thus far the books. A few hours of reading and I was full of facts, yet still completely ignorant. Interesting as the history of the dynasty was—Micah was indeed the regent; at his bar-mitzvah and marriage, which the Hipsters hoped to celebrate on the same day, he would officially be proclaimed Rebbe—it told me nothing about Micah's plans, nothing about what had been going on in the court since the death of the Elder Hipster two years before. What I had enjoyed most were the stories of the old man's mordant wit. For example:

Maase she-hoyo, a thing that really happened. The Hipster once had a penitent in the court, who, as is the way of penitents, forgot himself one night while playing his guitar and singing, and began to play the treyf abomination and hymn to the arch-patriarch of priests and filthy monks, rakhmone litslan, Dominicus. Hearing the then popular song pollute his holy house of study, the Hipster resolved to teach the penitent a lesson. Rather than hitting the young man or driving him from the bes-medresh (and thus from his new-found Judaism), the Hipster, a true bar mokhin ilo-in, a son of the supernal intelligences, grabbed the guitar and himself burst into song, to the same tune:

Dominique-a-nique-a-nique
Hot zikh gevalgert ibern land,
A tseylem in der hant;
I in kirkhe, i in kloyzl
Hot geret er nor fun yoyzl,
Hot geret er nor fun yoyzl,

adding, to the tune of the English "Good evening, friends," "*Git yontif*, pontiff." At that, the young man realized his error and returned immediately to the proper path. Indeed, we have the story from this very young man, today a thing of wonder in all Jewish communities in all our dispersions wherever we happen to find ourselves, that great man, the singing hasid, Rabbi Tashlum Moneybach.

But I gained little insight into Micah himself, and too much help from my parents I couldn't expect. Not only were they stupider than I was—my mother had never heard of a bitter vetch, and neither of them had the faintest idea that the Hipster Talmud Torah was a sham, a smokescreen to cover my taggings-after after Micah Mushmelon—but I have also to admit that my experience in Oykrei Horim was in perfect accord with my family's entire way of life. My father was known far and wide as the single worst yeshiva student ever to come out of Brooklyn. Not in the sense that he was ill-behaved—any sign of life would have been welcomed—rather, and it pains me to have to admit such a thing in public, but common knowledge cannot be construed as tale-bearing, nor speaking the truth as a violation of the fifth commandment, he was just plain stupid. Thick-skulled, boneheaded, peanut-brained. About as sharp as a shoehorn. And worse, like so many stupid people of my acquaintance—and in grade six you tend to meet a lot of them—he took his own slowness for deliberateness, for a cautious, impeccably fulcrumed ratiocination which could at once embrace and weigh every possibility inherent in a given situation.

Try going out to eat with this kind of sage. Even in a glatt-kosher restaurant, a deli, a Moishe's Mekhaye; go sit at a table for forty-five minutes while *your* progenitor, the determiner of your very sex sits there trying to decide whether to have pastrami or corned beef, or a piece kishka maybe; or perhaps the combination plate—"You see, son, this is what we scholars call a *pshore*, or compromise." Watch him as he begins waving his hairy fist above his head, clenching and unclenching the prehensile fingers, yelling, "Waiter, waiter," and, having lured the wretch tableside, asking him, "Tell me, what's a *tasty* meat you've got?" In a delicayentsentessen!

And friends? Did I mention that they had none? Did I need to? Who marries this kind of a bargain? Much as I loved my parents—a commandment is still a commandment—wrong as the accusations of Rabbi Lester Dean most certainly were (he described the kind of mother I *wanted* to have), I have but one thing to say: Not for nothing do they call the opportunity class at a Bais Yaakov school for orthodox girls "the cow palace"—and I ain't talking looks. My mother is, in fact, an unusually beautiful woman. Really. And if they would have taught her to shut her mouth at the same time they showed her how to take *khale*, she probably could have done all right. I mean, she never stopped. We had three telephones in the house, and I swear by everything holy that not only did she often carry on conversations on all of them at once, but—and perhaps more to the point—she did not know a single fact, beyond the names of her family and acquaintances, her own and my birthdates, and the *yortsaytn* of each and every sage listed on the Sages of Israel *Yortsayt* Calendar taped to the door of our dairy fridge. I believe this is called an idiot savant.

There was nothing actually *wrong* with me, but nobody noticed; my biggest social problem was that I was *theirs*. The rare few who didn't know of my parents and their reputation, a feat akin to never having heard of Times Square, thought I was weird, anyway, because I never let anybody into my house.

My father worked for the government, and I'm still not sure if this was good for the Jews.

What cannot be denied was my surprise when my father, having downed four or five slivovitzes and given a command performance of "*Shikker iz a goy*," lurched into my room unannounced and asked me, since I was about to begin my new academic career at the Hipster Talmud Torah, whether I had ever heard of Micah Mushmelon. I had switched off my flashlight and pushed my still unread comic deep under the covers as soon as I heard footsteps outside my door, so I drowsily played dumb.

"You'll be meeting him for sure," my father informed me, tsk-tsking and clucking his tongue. "An unfortunate product of suburban living. They say that he's obsessed with the death of his parents, that he's delved into kabbala, practical kabbala, I mean, to try and solve the riddle of their murder. The old Hipster told him simply to accept it as the will of God, as a sort of payment to him for leaving Europe before the War, when men of his calibre were needed there. But it didn't have much effect on the kid. He's a genius, but a little bit strange. Reads too many books. You just stick to your studies. I was no bookworm and I'm doing plenty all-right.

"Anyway, after the old man died a couple of years ago, they say the kid got even crazier. Thinks the whole thing—his parents, any accident on the street, even the old man's dying—is part of some giant plot, don't ask me against what. The Hipster Rebbe was at least a hundred years old; who'd have to kill him, the way he used to smoke?

"What I wanna tell you, though"—my father used to walk exactly the way he talked—"All I wanna tell you, is to keep away from him. Genius or no genius, there's something about that kid that I don't like. He's too ugly."

"You know him, then?" I asked.

"Not personally, but I've heard enough to know that he's no good for a good boy like you."

I didn't know if there was really a plot against Micah Mushmelon or not, but I was beginning to hope that there was; this plot against my parents was already starting to be fun. Instead of feeling guilty, I was proud of myself. They would never have done anything like this.

"Oh, by the way," my father said on his way out, "hurry up with that *Khamoro Kadisho* comic. I wanna find out what happens."

"SHRAGA-GETSL SAID SOMETHING ABOUT I'd have to take my clothes off, like? That you needed me naked?" I was still worried about advertising my covenant with the Lord.

Micah Mushmelon threw back his head as far as anyone without a neck can do so and roared with laughter. "You'd make one heck of a *mikve* toy at that," he said, "but that isn't what he meant by 'a naked Shraga'."

What he *had* meant, we'd get to later. "Don't worry. There's nothing like a couple days *yontef* for a good Torah bootcamp."

God or fate—which are one and the same—or Micah Mushmelon himself—close, but no Signor, as the *Times* would put it—had so arranged things that our initial meeting fell out on a Wednesday, two days after Yom Kippur. *Sukkes*, the Festival of Tabernacles, was set to begin Friday night, and no religious school operates over the eight days of the festival, half of which (the first and final two days) are official holidays, i.e., *yontef*, anyway, with the middle four being semi-holidays. *Khol hamoyed*, as they are called, the profane part of the appointed time; while work as such is permitted, it is considered meritorious to refrain from it if at all possible. In order to facilitate orientation into my new "school," Shraga-Getsl had suggested to my parents that it might be a good idea if I were to spend the holiday at the Hipster house of study. I could meet the "other boys," and even sleep in their *sukke*. Still under the influence of Shraga-Getsl's flattery—he had indeed known my grandfather back in Plotsk; "worst yeshiva boy in the history of the town," he told me—my parents had acquiesced easily. My mother packed me a bag, fixed me a lunch and reminded me that today was the anniversary of the death of the holy Rebbe of Dlugaszow, may his merits protect us, and sent her "big boy, going away just like a real yeshiva *bokher* in the old country" on his three blocks' journey to the Hipster HQ.

I found Mushmelon sitting in his study, chewing the nub of a licorice pipe and reading a pamphlet of his grandfather on the meaning of *Sukkes*. "Come over here, Potasznik." Not for Micah Mushmelon the empty forms of conventional discourse. "Licorice pipe?" he offered.

"No, thanks. My dentist says no."

"Dentists," he sighed. "Hypocrites with honeyed smiles, the praises of God in their throats and a double-edged sword in their hands. They look into the mouths of women and emerge to give us counsel. Did I run off to one after you knocked my tooth out? I offered thanks to the Lord who thus spared his servant yet another potential encounter with the cursed race of traducers. If the Lord approved of the dentistry, he wouldn't have given us an Oral Law. Keep the Torah in your mouth and the cuspid-*hakkers* out."

I took a pipe.

"Good, eh?" he asked, smiling.

"Edenic," I answered with a cough. I dropped the filling into my shirt pocket and asked about my nudity.

"I'm glad to have found you on *Sukkes*," he continued, after putting my fears to rest. "It's our national holiday, so to speak, for it was on a *Sukkes* just like this one many years ago that my sainted grandfather completed the development of his system."

He went on before I could ask him how; no power on earth can stop a Mushmelon anecdote, once begun. "During his residence at the first New Hipst, the one in Idaho"—he seemed to take it for granted that I had done my homework—"my grandfather set himself the task of learning English. *Treyfer* than Polish, he said, it couldn't be. There being no native speakers among his following at that time, he obtained a dictionary, a grammar and a few novels by Charles Dickens. He made rapid progress, so much so that he shortly took out a subscription to the local newspaper, in which he one day saw an advertisement for a concert by the Mormon Tabernacle Choir. As the word Mormon did not appear in his dictionary, my grandfather construed it as a place name; tabernacle, he already knew, meant a *sukke*.

" 'Amerike gonif,' he thought. 'What won't they think of next?' Although he'd never heard of a *sukke* choir his whole time in Europe, the idea struck his fancy, and he wrote off to the choir, inquiring as to whether they'd like to appear in New Hipst over *khol ha-moyed Sukkes*.

"As the choir disembarked from its train, my grandfather was rather dismayed to notice a large number of women. For the choir he didn't mind paying, but that they should *shlep* with their wives, this was going a little too far. And the men—where were their beards? Where was the image of God? He approached an official-looking gentleman. The man understood not a word of Yiddish. A Frenk, perhaps, a Sephardi? He knew no Hebrew, but asked quickly enough in English what was the meaning of that big shack on the other side of the tracks, the one with the branches on the roof; the Mormon Tabernacle Choir was not about to lodge in a cow-stall or lean-to.

" *'Ot dus iz ayer sukke, ayer* tabernacle.'

"The man smiled politely, as one does at incomprehensible foreigners. 'And a tabernacle is not by you a *sukke*?' my grandfather asked.

" 'Sir, I have no idea what you're talking about. Are you sure,' he asked, looking my grandfather over bemusedly, 'that you're really Mormons?'

" 'Mormons? *Vi kenen mir zayn* Mormons? You're from Mormon, we're from Hipst.'

" 'We, sir, are from Salt lake City.'

" 'Yeah, so? I figured Mormon was a neighbourhood.'

" 'Mormon is the popular designation for us members of the Church of Jesus Christ of Latter Day Saints,' the choir-leader replied with some little self-satisfaction.

" 'The what from who?!' screamed my grandfather. 'Here in New Hipst *watcht men his mouth!'*

"The choir-master wasn't entirely stupid, thank God, so they managed to avoid a pogrom. 'You people, I take it, are members of the Hebrew faith celebrating your festival of Tabernacles, or Sukkoth, as I believe you call it?'

" *'Azoy,'* said my grandfather. 'And you people are not?'

" 'Are not. Something about our name, the tabernacle and all, must have given you the wrong impression.'

" 'You're darn tootin. *Vey gevald,* what's gonna be?'

"It wasn't so hard to figure. The Hipsters put the Mormons up for the night, and the rumours began to fly. 'Hipsters receive Missionaries,' read the headline in *The Torah Panorama;* a group of Lithuanian zealots from Montana burned a Star of David at the gate to New Hipst. My grandfather sent letters to all the appropriate persons and institutions explaining the nature of his error, and got the Momons to do likewise. The whole incident was soon forgotten—by everybody but my grandfather and his followers. 'Praise God,' he exclaimed, 'that we've lived to see the day when I make a mistake, that my flock might realize that I have followed faithfully in the path of my fathers and remained a simpleton.'

"And it's from this incident, Potasznik, that he derived the name of all Hipster institutions the world over: Shoymer Pesoyim, Protector of Idiots; from this that my grandfather arrived at his revolutionary doctrine of what you don't know *will* hurt you, and led him to insist on a secular education for all his followers. So *khol ha-moyed Sukkes* of every year in turn, the Hipsters gather here, at what we call Rosh Pesoyim, the Head of Idiots, and present academic papers in their chosen disciplines and fields. The selection this year looks unusually good. I'd especially recommend the paper on 'Brooklyn Dodgers: *Shokling* styles in present-day New York.' I think it'll be a doozy."

"But what about the danger?" I cried. "Their faith could be disturbed."

Mushmelon snorted. "It didn't hurt the Rambam none, did it?"

"But he was the Rambam."

"And I am the Mushmelon. Maimonides didn't become the Rambam for a good long time after he was already defunct. Before that, he was just some guy whose books you could burn whenever you wanted ... And remember, Potasznik, my grandfather never intended for everybody to be a Hipster hasid. That's why we don't have a Talmud Torah. You have to join as an adult, even if your parents are already Hipsters. The renovation of the world is not a job for children."

"Then what do you need me for? What about *my* secular education?"

"You're special, Potasznik; you don't know how special. And as for your schooling, you'll soon find out that just knowing me is a liberal education."

"And you," I asked, summoning all my courage, "How'd you get so smart? You sit here talking about grown-ups and academic papers and remaking the world, and you don't even count for a *minyan* where they give girls *aliyes*. Maybe I'm special and maybe I'm not, but how'd you get to be such a star out of Jacob?"

Mushmelon giggled, stuck a new licorice pipe in his mouth. He chewed contemplatively for a minute or two, drumming his fingers on the now closed volume. I was expecting him to summon Shraga-Getsl to break my neck. Fine thing—last night, a scholarship student; today, thrown out of a school that wasn't even there and maybe even maimed for good.

"I'm glad you asked, Potasznik. Do not misread my silence; some things aren't easy to explain." He took another bite of his pipe. I started breathing again. "Tell me, do you know what you were doing before you were born?"

"Learning in yeshiva, like everybody else," I answered.

"Yes, in the heavenly yeshiva. Under the final supervision of Moses our Teacher. And what did you learn there?"

"Everything, I guess."

"Everything?"

"Well, you know. The whole Torah, the whole *gemore* with all its commentaries. The whole written law and the whole oral law."

"Um-humm." Mushmelon nodded and pulled at a sidelock. "And you only guess?" he asked, pushing the *dashikl* back towards the crown of his head. "Don't you remember?"

"Why should I remember? Everybody knows that before you're born an angel gives you a *shnel*, a little tap, right here," and I indicated the space directly below my septum and above my upper lip, which my mother referred to as "the cutest little dimple in the whole wide world," "and you forget everything."

"*Azoy*," said Micah Mushmelon. "Now what would you say, Potasznik, if I were to tell you that I remember you from the heavenly yeshiva, that we shared a desk there, and that you excelled in *khakire*, in meticulous investigation?"

"Give me a pipe ... please." My voice covered three octaves in the course of the sentence. "You mean to tell me ...?"

"That's right," he said with an air of finality, "I never got hit."

I swallowed the pipe whole. Mushmelon rang frantically for Shraga-Getsl, who raced in and began slapping me on the back like I'd just had a boy, while Micah Mushmelon pumped my arms up and down. Shraga-Getsl picked me up and applied the Heimlich manoeuvre. Soon as I could breathe again, Shraga-Getsl exited, returning a moment later with a pitcher of water—"Drink," he told me—and a large plate of *kugel*; "in honour of the Dlugaszower Rebbe's *yortsayt*," he explained.

Mushmelon waited for him to leave before resuming his discourse. "What would you say if I were to tell you further that there is not only a yeshiva in heaven, but a graduate school as well?"

I asked him what a graduate school was, and he explained. "And I never got a *shnel* for it, either. My grandfather was not without influence in those circles, and he arranged for me to avoid the tap legally. I know he was a true *tsaddik*, for I can remember seeing him in heaven almost every night. He told Rabbi Yokhanan ben Dahabai about the *Kama-Sutra*; he showed Rabbi Judah the Prince, the Holy Teacher, that the words of *Adoyn Oylom* scan perfectly to the chorus of *Glow Worm*. My unmolested birth was the price demanded.

"The case went before the heavenly court, the angel Paskiel presiding. Arguments were brought pro and con; the jury deliberated a mere five minutes. 'A deal is a deal,' they proclaimed. 'As the rabbis couldn't go down and learn this stuff themselves, they have no basis on which to appeal. The child walks.'

"And so I did—with a world's worth of knowledge, all of it the absolute truth, none of it ever to be forgotten. Should I seem to you arrogant once in a while, should I appear to boast, remember, Shraga"—this was the first time he'd called me Shraga. A lump still rises in my throat when I recall it—"remember, Shraga, that it's really my grandfather whom I praise."

I told him that I'd never forget.

IV

THE FOLLOWING DAY AND A HALF was swallowed up in a whirlpool of instruction and observance. With *Shabbes* and *Sukkes* coinciding, with hasidic academics arriving from all corners of the world, the atmosphere around the Hipster *besmedresh* was one of peculiar intensity, a cross between a pilgrimage and a job interview. Micah Mushmelon began to impart to me the rudiments of his philosophical system, assuring me that by the time the holiday was over I'd have absorbed enough to put it to use. To what use, he still had not revealed, save to confide to me that the whole future of the Hebrew race depended upon our activities.

The restoration of my own soul to its pristine glory and grandeur, to the specialness he'd already mentioned, was, I realized, at least part of his mission. "I've come to fetch you, Potasznik. You have no idea how close we once were, and I'm not about to let an old friendship die. Remember, in heaven we had no names. Shraga-Getsl and I have spent years tracing the path of your soul, and it's only the merest accident—as if there were any such thing—that placed you within three blocks of us. I mean to unblock your mind, Potasznik. Slowly, to be sure, but thoroughly. To undo the effects of the angel's tap. For, you see, I know the secret of remembrance. *'Zukhoyr al tishkakh,'* it says in the Torah, 'Remember, do not forget'—by me, this is a positive commandment all by itself."

We spoke and we read; he questioned and I answered. He questioned again, and I answered correctly. We went together to the Hipster *mikve* in preparation for the Sabbath and holiday.

I noticed two *sukkes* in the yard of the Hipster edifice. Shraga-Getsl informed me that one was the general *sukke*, where Micah Mushmelon would preside later that night, and that the other was Micah Mushmelon's personal *sukke* where he would sleep and receive those of his followers who wished a private audience. "You," he said, "will sleep in the little one."

I felt as if I had come home. Especially after Micah Mushmelon explained to me that I had absolutely no biological connection with my parents. "They are a punishment," he declared, something even I could have told him a long, long time before. "You were supposed to have been born to Allen Ginsberg, the homosexual, beatnik, Buddhist poet, as the result of an interlude with a woman. Your example was to have served to return him to the ways of nature and his people. But you acted up one day in heaven, and without meaning to, hit Shammai with a spitball."

"*The* Shammai?" I asked, incredulous that my name should even appear in the same sentence with that of the sage. "The Shammai from *bays Hillel* and *bays Shammai*, from the schools of Hillel and Shammai? The Shammai who chased away the *shaygets* who wanted to learn the whole Torah while the *shaygets* was standing on one foot, so the *shaygets* went to Hillel and he taught it to him?"

"That Shammai."

"But he has the worst temper in the whole *gemore*."

"Not just in the *gemore*. Soon as he caught you, he arranged for you to be born to the dumbest couple he could find, and had you dispatched thither forthwith. You're lucky you only got him in the back—he could have had you sent to absolute *goyim*, you know."

"Then there's no hereditary taint?"

"None at all."

"*Borukh ha-shem.*" *Erev-Sukkes* of that year I became a free man. "By the way," I asked Micah, "With my real father, what's his name …?"

"Ginsberg."

"Yeah. What's a homosexual?" I knew the word from crossword puzzles as "loving its own kind," which I was pretty sure meant a philanthropic Jew.

"*Freg nisht,*" he told me. "Don't ask."

The singing and dancing that night, the table-pounding and ritualized bonding, were unlike anything I'd ever seen or even heard of. The hasidim conga'd about the courtyard for hours, singing *Yibone Beys-Ha-Mikdosh*, May the Temple Be Rebuilt, to the standard conga tune, but the real climax came at what Micah told me they called simply "*Dem Rebns Nign,*" "The Rebbe's Tune," referring, of course, to the old Hipster. Although he had written neither words nor music, the combination of the two had become so closely identified with him that even without the confines of Hipst the song was known as "*Dem Hipster Rebns Nign.*" From the stroke of midnight, and continuing until four in the morning, the hasidim snaked about the courtyard in an s-shaped line, doing a slow drag to the tune, Micah told me, of "Flat Foot Floogie," singing the sixth verse of the hundred and sixteenth Psalm in Hebrew: "The Lord protects the idiots; I went down low and he saved me," the Hipster theme-verse.

At each repetition of "I went down low," the hasid then at the head of the line had to pass under a limbo bar held by Shraga-Getsl and another assistant, while the rest of the line dipped as drastically as they could. *Not a single hasid was ever seen to fall.* If the hasid succeeded in passing under the bar, the line remained shuffling in place, while he returned to his spot and made another attempt, Shraga-Getsl and his helper having lowered the bar somewhat. Each continued until he failed, then took his place at the back of the line while the next hasid went through the same routine.

They were some good limboers, those hasidim of Hipst; every hasid made at least two passes, and some of them, their capotes thrown off, their hats deposited atop the hat of the man directly behind them, went down so low, I would have thought an envelope would have trouble getting under the bar.

Micah took no part in any of this, sitting instead at the head of the courtyard and watching his flock, much as an engine remains stationary while turning the wheels of a vehicle. "*Gib a kik*, Potasznik, at what my *zeyde* hath wrought. Each one of them goes down to the very depths, but with joy and song; each finally arises to realize that his success has made him the last, the last and least of all his brethren; that his own achievement is only for the sake of his own self-denial, in order that another may yet be first. This is a mystery of mysteries and a secret of secrets; if I were but slighter of build," he continued, taking another piece of *kugel*, "and sharper of ear—I'm tone-deaf, you know; I cannot do everything—I would be more than happy to join them myself."

"And what about me?" I asked, pleading. "When do I get to dance?"

"After you're bar-mitzvah," he replied, "and not a day before." I had forgotten that with the possible exception of Micah himself, there were no children in the Hipster court, and I realized then how great an honour was being bestowed upon me. I had already earned my acceptance.

Much to my surprise, I discovered the next morning that the Hipster services were very much like those of hasidim everywhere. Men were chosen to lead the prayers by virtue of age and learning; as in most such synagogues, the cantor was inaudible except when he coughed, and was usually at the bottom of, say, page forty-three when you were at the top of page thirty-eight. The entire Saturday morning service, including the special and rather lengthy insertions in honour of *Sukkes*, was over in about ninety minutes. "We don't go for all this crying and *shraying*," Micah told me. "To us, prayer is an urgent dispatch; God needs his praise, as if it's possible, and we, *nebekh*, need our sundry deliverances—now. When you send a telegram, you can the adjectives and get to the point. Same with our *davening*. We put it down, and He picks it up."

While the hasidim filed out the back of the *bes-medresh* and into the *sukke*, Micah led me around to the front of the building. "We'll get him some air," he said, but instead of the Sabbath calm we were expecting, we walked straight into, I don't know, the beginnings of a riot or the flight from a natural disaster. Hundreds, thousands of Jews of every age, from every community, were running frantically through the streets, wailing and tearing their hair as if observing a witches' *Shabbes*. Only their repeated keening—"on account of our sins, because of our many transgressions"—spoke of anything other than a deliberate violation of the day. Micah and I hadn't budged from the doorway of the *bes-medresh*, afraid lest we, too, be caught up

in the frenzy of transgression: running, hair-pulling, lamenta-
tion—all are forbidden on the Sabbath. Micah folded his hands
over the top of his *dashikl*—he looked for all the world like one
of those big round balls little kids sit on top of and hop around
on—and shouted into the crowd, *"Shabbes, yidn!* Remember the
holy *Shabbes! Shabbes un yontef,* you can't be sad. It's *zman
simkhaseynu,* the season of our joy, so what's going on here,
where's the problem?"

"Problem?" someone shouted back. "Who's got a problem?
We got no problem; we're as happy as Christians in a brewery.
Just because they found Rabbi Wasserfoygl and his four sons
dead in their *sukke,* why shouldn't we be happy?"

Micah and I stared at each other, too shocked to speak.
"Rabbi Wasserfoygl, you say?" he asked again.

"The very same. In the multitude of our sins, the Lord had
him and his sons murdered in their *sukke* sometime last night.
His wife found them this morning."

"Blessed be the righteous judge," the two of us exclaimed in
unison. "Murdered?" I asked. "You say they were murdered?"

"Vu-den, what else? Five healthy young men and God have
mercy boys should all decide to have a heart attack at once?
What else could it be?"

"They found maybe a weapon?" Micah wanted to know.

"They found maybe nothing. Five bodies without a mark.
Nothing taken. The bedsheets not even rumpled." The man was
starting to cry. He looked to be in his early seventies, sere and
bent as last year's *lulav.* I could almost hear him creaking as
he wept. "There's no screaming on *Shabbes,* but we're screaming anyway. *Pikuakh nefesh,* the saving of a life, pushes the
Shabbes away, and it looks as if the I-haven't-washed-my-hands
means to do us all a deed. So we're doing just like the Ninevites

after Jonah gave them the warning: the Trebitscher Rebbe has already declared Monday a fast, and so has the Litvak board of rabbis." The Trebitscher Rebbe was the most powerful Hungarian Rebbe in town, and that meant the most powerful Rebbe, period. Usually, if he said *treyf*—and he always said *treyf*—the Litvaks said kosher. If they could publicly agree on anything—and there was no sign of the Messiah—then the Holy One, Blessed Be He, must have had it in for us for sure.

"To the private *sukke*, Potasznik. We have work to do."

I didn't want to do anything but cry. Rabbi Elyakim Wasserfoygl had been Supreme Commander and Executive Strategic Secretary of Oykrei Horim, the organization from which I had been expelled the previous summer. He was known as a friend of children and was beloved of all mankind. Had he not been so modest, had he not framed the Oykrei Horim constitution in such a way as deliberately to enhance the power and prestige of the General Secretary and Company Commander, Rabbi Dean, I have no doubt but that I would have been vindicated and my rank restored. What greater testimony can there be to the man than that I still loved him, even after what had happened to me? What finer example of humanity could be found than a man who would establish such an organization, bear the burdens of its foundation and clear it a path to Torah and good deeds, and then virtually hand the entire structure, even the keys, to a struggling young rabbi, merely to help him get started? Rabbi Wasserfoygl was a saint; Rabbi Dean was Rabbi Dean, and I never confused him with Wasserfoygl. Dean's being wrong had no effect on the purity of Rabbi Wasserfoygl and his vision.

And now he was dead. He and his four sons. They were all older than I, two were even married, and I had known them only by sight. But he was dead. I felt as if I had been orphaned twice in the space of three months. Rabbi Wasserfoygl was the Aaron of our day, loving all and loved by them in return. Pole and Hungarian, hasid and Litvak, religious and even secular—all alike regarded Elyakim Wasserfoygl as the embodiment, the *shpitz* and very zenith of Torah Jewry, and all alike regarded his death and the extirpation of his seed as a portent of looming ill. Even Micah Mushmelon was blowing his nose.

He popped a chick-pea into his mouth—his holy fist would not even close about a licorice pipe on the Sabbath—and slammed his bulk into a chair. "Ruined! All my plans—for nought! Whether you like it or not, Shraga, your training period has come to an end. *He* has anticipated me, even more foully than I would have expected."

"He? Who he?"

Mushmelon ignored me. "We must start now. Our hand must be raised in action, and that action must be completed before the end of *Sukkes*, or I fear there will never be another *Sukkes* again." He pondered a moment, slowly chewing a mouthful of chick-peas. "Of course!" he cried out, a bit of chick-pea lodging on my gabardine. "On top of everything else, he picked this day as a deliberate affront to us, to me, to the memories of my sainted parents and grandfather."

"But who is he, Micah? Who are you talking about and what is he doing?"

"Whom."

"Huh?"

"Whom are you talking about. You couldn't make these errors if you'd speak Yiddish."

"OK. *Fin vemen reydsti?*"

"That's better. Let me ask you a question, Potasznik. How long were you a member of Oykrei Horim?"

"About a year," I said. "Maybe a little more. I joined as soon as it started and stayed there until I got kicked out over the summer."

"So, fourteen months, more or less?" I nodded. Micah Mushmelon hummed. "I'm going to explain something and I want you to pay attention. Rabbi Wasserfoygl was indeed murdered, as the man on the street surmised. And this was no random killing, no blind hooliganism. Do you know how many kids there are in Oykrei Horim?" I guessed that he and I were probably the only boys under the age of thirteen not to belong to the organization, and so far as the Bnos Khayil, the Daughters of Valour, which was the girls' auxiliary went, I was sure that every girl in the city, except maybe the Torah Sluts, was a member in good standing.

"Precisely." Micah gave me a sour look. "And don't ever say Torah Sluts to me again." I sometimes forgot that he was sort of a grown-up, and talked to him as if he were just another kid. "Rabbi Wasserfoygl's genius was that everything he did was pure Torah, with no room for arguments or disputes. Unmediated Sinai, apparent to all. In another ten years, he could have changed the face of *yidishkayt*, could have produced a generation entirely worthy. And you know what that means?"

"*Meshiekhs tsaytn*," I answered. "The Messiah would come."

"Correct. And do you remember what it says about when *meshiekh's* going to come?"

"To a generation either entirely worthy or entirely guilty, which means utterly sinful."

"Good. And can the latter condition ever come to pass?"

"No. There will always be a saving remnant of the righteous."

"Well done, Potasznik, although in this case I'd hardly call it a *saving* remnant. Nevertheless, you've got the general idea."

"You mean then that Rabbi Wasserfoygl was killed by somebody who doesn't want *meshiekh* to come?" I was incredulous—who didn't want *meshiekh*?

"Exactly." Micah took his finger from his nose and pointed in the general direction of the street. "There is a man out there who wants to keep us in exile, who wants the world to remain unfulfilled—*aftselakhis*, simply out of spite. And it is to fighting this man that I have devoted my life and energies, that I have enlisted your aid. The murder of Rabbi Wasserfoygl was but one step in his latest campaign for world domination; we have days, perhaps only hours—and then, too late."

"But who is he? What is he up to and where will we find him?"

"Imagine, Potasznik, imagine if you will a being completely of 'the other side,' a man with the brain of Asmodeus and the beard of Old Man Mose; the heart of a stoat and the soul of … of"—he began hissing in a breathless rush—"What happened in the Pardes?"

"Four went into the Pardes, the private garden of mysticism. Ben Azzaai looked and died; Ben Zoma looked and flipped; another one looked and became a heretic; and Rabbi Akiva went in and came out in safety."

"And 'another one', who was he?"

"Can I say it?"

"Go ahead, this isn't *kheyder* here."

"Elisha ben Avuyah, may the name of the wicked rot."

"Exactly. The soul of Elisha ben Avuyah, masquerading as a learned and pious Jew."

"But he's been dead like two thousand years already."

" 'I never died,' says he. Bodies die, Potasznik. All the rest is heresy."

"So there's somebody running around who's the reincarnation of Elisha ben Avuyah, may the name—"

"*Genig shoyn*, enough already."

"And he's the guy who killed Rabbi Wasserfoygl?"

"Absolutely correct. Only you forgot one detail: he's an acquaintance, maybe once an intimate of yours."

You could have given me a root canal. "A friend of mine?" I asked. "But I don't have any friends!" Micah Mushmelon frowned. "Except you."

"I didn't say a friend, I said an acquaintance. Somebody you probably wish you'd never met."

"Somebody eleven years old?" I asked incredulously.

"Think back a few months. Remember your court-martial? Who initiated the proceedings?"

"Rabbi Dean."

"Who was the chief witness against you?"

"Rabbi Dean."

"And the judge who condemned you?"

Once again I said, "Rabbi Dean."

"Rab-bi De-an." He stretched the words over the better part of a minute. "Who poisoned your precious candy, poured Coca-Cola into kosher mikves? Rabbi Dean," he shouted, "Rabbi Lester Dean, better known as Les Dean, The World's Greatest *Apikoyros*, The Manischewitz of Crime."

All I can remember is teetering backwards in my chair.

V

WHEN I CAME TO, Shraga-Getsl was waving a schmaltz herring under my nose. "Here," he said as I opened my eyes, "eat this." After I had licked the bones clean, he put me back in my chair. Micah handed me a Mayim Khayim cola and bade me drink.

In the brief time I'd spent under Micah's tutelage, I'd learned one thing at least. So despite my grogginess, despite the ache in my head and the rent in my heart, I started talking before he could decide whether I was really awake. I knew it could be my last chance. "Nobody hates Rabbi Dean more than I do," I said, "but I just don't see how he's responsible for all the evil in the world. He's a rabbi! And the other kids seem to like him enough. Even when I was still in Oykrei Horim I didn't, but mostly because he always ignored me."

"So because he's a rabbi, he can't be evil, is that it?" Micah asked. Shraga-Getsl snorted.

"Well, he keeps the *mitsves*, he *davens*, holds *Shabbes*. He knows a ton of *gemore*—*gants shas*, the whole thing by heart. If he didn't believe anything, why would he learn like that? The whole world thinks he's a *sheyner yid*, a beautiful Jew. Rabbi Wasserfoygl trusted him with everything."

"And look what happened to Rabbi Wasserfoygl. You think he's such a *sheyner yid*, you think beauty has anything to do with it?" He waved dismissively and cleared his throat. "Hate the *goyim* as you might, Potasznik, it cannot be denied." He slammed his fist onto the table, leaned so far forward that I could smell the chick-peas on his breath, and stuffed his mouth again. "No, it cannot be denied that the Germans, the very incarnation of evil on this green earth"—he'd already said that Les Dean was, but even I could see the difference—"it cannot be denied that the Germans had the neatest uniforms in World War Two."

I'd long harboured such a suspicion myself, and was glad I wasn't the only one. "But how does that affect Rabbi Dean?"

"Les Dean!" he screamed. "Forget the rabbi."

"But …"

"*Sapienti sat*, Potsy. *Sapienti sat*. Aesthetics, as we know, has no moral value. *La Belle Dame Sans Merci* and all that. Who'd you rather hang out with, me or Nastassja Kinski?"

"*Sapienti sat?*"

"Latin, Shraga, for *dai le-meyven*. Just because Les Dean looks like a holy rabbi, doesn't mean he is one."

"I don't know," I said. "You're going to have to prove it. You can't just go around accusing rabbis of murder."

Micah Mushmelon, Boy Talmudist, leaned back in his chair and sighed like an aged *kheyder* teacher whom the class can't figure out. "It's not your fault, I suppose. Had we had a chance to finish your training, this would all be clear to you by now." He gestured to Shraga-Getsl, who slid a sheaf of tiny papers wrapped round with a black ribbon from the sleeve of his capote and handed them to Micah. "If you don't believe me, take a few minutes to look over *The Black Book,* then make up your own mind. Meanwhile, I have matters to attend to in the house."

They left me alone in the *sukke* with a half-filled bowl of chick-peas. The papers were small, the size of a pocket calendar, and covered with a calligraphic, scribal Hebrew of the sort used in mezuzas and *tefillin*, the better to stress the importance of the contents and, as Shraga-Getsl told me later, the easier to hide the volume. "I have a false pair of *tefillin* where I keep them during the week. *Shabbes* and *yontef*, I wear the whole bunch tied around my elbow." As he rarely left the building or its courtyard on these occasions, there was no problem of carrying involved.

As I read through the densely printed pages, I realized that my life had been lived in cloud cuckooland, in a mirage of safety, security and order in which everything proceeded the way it was supposed to. I had had no idea that Les Dean was practically running the world, that he had such influence on almost everything that happened. But the words of *The Black Book* could not be denied:

THESE ARE THE GENERATIONS OF LES DEAN [read the pamphlet], age and true name unknown, place of birth a mystery, his parentage as obscure as his villainy is renowned. HEAR, O ISRAEL and BE APPALLED, YE SKIES! He himself has boasted that the soul of the heretical Other lives within him; he himself has claimed that by the age of seven he was riding the subway on Saturdays, except on Purim. He fasts on *Simkhes Toyre*, eats *treyf* all year except on Yom Kipper and the ninth of Av, when he prepares himself a feast of gefilte fish, chicken soup, *kugel* and other typical Jewish dishes.

He is Jeroboam ben Nevat, A SINNER AND ONE WHO BRINGS THE MULTITUDE TO SIN. In the guise of a *kashrus* inspector, he poured pigs'-foot jelly into the ingredients of a popular and well-known kosher children's confection; he likes to jog in Jewish neighbourhoods, work up a good sweat, then repair to a nearby synagogue, where he rubs his sweaty palms over a Torah-scroll, thus erasing a letter and rendering the scroll void. And always on last week's portion.

He has FOUND FACES OF THE TORAH THAT ARE NOT ACCORDING TO THE LAW; he has twisted the saying THOU HAST CHOSEN US in the following manner: if the L-rd has chosen us, and making any sort of selection or choice is forbidden on the Sabbath and Festivals; if He chose us by giving us the Torah; and if he gave us the Torah on *Shavues;* then we, the Children of Israel, are all *muktse,* forbidden to be touched on the Sabbath etc., for such observance implies a separation of soul from body. And it says in Leviticus, AND YOU SHALL LIVE BY THEM; says Rashi, AND NOT DIE; and as we all know, the preservation of a life voids the Sabbath. And so, in choosing us, the L-rd has instructed us explicitly to disregard and ignore the Sabbath.

WOE TO THE EYES THAT READ THIS! We will not multiply examples.

Les Dean bears a particular animus against the holy community of Hipst, the living contradiction of all his claims to a progressive conservatism. The copy of *As a Driven Leaf* [the title was translated into Hebrew], a scabrous and sympathetic novelization of the life of the cursed Other, MAY THE NAME OF THE WICKED ROT, left beside the lifeless, murdered body of Rabbi S.B. Mushmelon, MAY SUCH A THING NEVER BEFALL US, was a virtual admission of his guilt, a mocking challenge: Try and catch me. CAN THE ETHIOPIAN CHANGE HIS SKIN OR THE LEOPARD HIS SPOTS? No, but Les Dean, The World's Greatest *Apikoyros*, changes one appearance and identity for another as doth the lickerish secularist his prophylactics. He is seen, but never captured; heard of, but never in time.

Has he not pioneered the Esther Williams discount *mikve* and invented the Jack-in-the-box *tefillin?* Each phylactery, G-D PRESERVE US, has a lever attached to its side. One gives the lever a turn, the phylactery plays the Israeli national anthem, and at the end of the first verse there leaps forth from the phylactery of your choice a Jack-in-the-box, wearing a capote, a round sable hat (*shtrayml*, in the language of Germany), a mini-prayer shawl and holding a tiny banner on which is written, "*Shma Yisruel,* you can drive to *shul.*"

WOE AND WIND TO THE EYES THAT SEE THIS!

The Day before his death, the Hipster Rebbe, MAY THE MEMORY OF THE RIGHTEOUS AND HOLY BE FOR A BLESSING, found an Andy Williams record in a Cootie Williams sleeve—and did David the King not say, THEY STILL BRING FORTH FRUIT IN SENESENCE. How then could he have died of old age?

And the rest of the deeds of Les Dean, The World's Greatest ...

Twelve more leaves of this, and I was wishing that Les Dean had apostasized *in gantsn;* as an *apikoyros,* he was constrained to overturn the tables, to upend and subvert the laws. A real *apikoyros* is no *goysiher kop,* how much more so the world's greatest; he had to maintain a complete, accurate knowledge of Torah and Torah Judaism. The *apikoyros* doesn't simply reject; he has to destroy, and in the name of absolutely nothing.

My heart crumbled like matzoh as I read of his murder of Micah Mushmelon's family; the deeds of Les Dean were horseradish to my eyes, my tears stained the pages on which they were written: murder, seduction, he even had a tattoo of a naked woman on his chest, in flesh-coloured ink so it wouldn't show in the *mikve.* The only good he could do was inadvertent, a grudging trade-off for the sake of some greater evil: he had infiltrated every organization dedicated to the construction of the third Temple before the advent of the Messiah, simply to afford himself an opportunity of violating the laws of sacrifice, no matter in how specious a fashion.

"So what," I wondered aloud, "does he want with Oykrei Horim?"

"Can't you see, Potasznik?" said Micah Mushmelon, waddling back into the *sukke.* "Oykrei Horim is the chance he's been waiting for, an opportunity to corrupt an entire generation, not just a few pathetic individuals. And after he's swung all the children over, what more natural target than a congregation with no room for children, than his oldest living enemy?" I gasped. He nodded. "That's right, the Holy Congregation of Hipst. And when you're talking Hipst, you're talking me."

Him. The last link in the Hipster chain. "With the Hipsters out of the way, with no Jewish alternative but a third-rate Europe in the middle of Brooklyn, Les Dean will have an open field … People have laughed at my appearance; I *chose* this body, Shraga, for I knew before my birth that I was destined to be … a bulwark, the last bulwark against *apikorses* and plain bad taste. I'll tell you something that's not in the book." His voice dropped to a whisper. "Les Dean's favourite singer is Pete Seeger."

"Because he garbled the words to *Tsena Tsena* the way Les Dean seeks to garble the Torah?" I stated more than asked.

Micah Mushmelon ran over and kissed me. "Now you're catching on."

"And then life will be nothing but …"

"Politically correct. He believes in intermarriage between species. When his first wife died, he made invalid *tefillin* out of her."

"He really is The World's Greatest *Apikoyros*," I said.

"And the Manischewitz of Crime," added Micah. "Everybody knows that there are plenty of kosher food companies, but still, when you think of kosher food, you think Manischewitz. The same with Les Dean. There are plenty of criminals in this world, and *apikorsim* without number; but when you think of an *apikoyros*, you think of Les Dean."

With my head aswim, my reason near overpowered under the burden of the recent revelations, "Can he be stopped?" I asked.

"He can and he will, or my name isn't Micah Mushmelon, Boy Talmudist."

VI

OUR FIRST ITEM OF BUSINESS was to get a look at the fatal *sukke*.
"The police will undoubtedly have removed the bodies by
now," said Micah. "Probably Jewish policemen, too," he sighed.
"But I'm sure that they've overlooked most of the real clues.
Only a trained *talmid khokhem* or disciple of the wise is capable
of elucidating a *dovar ha-lomeyd me-inyonoy*, a matter cleared up
by its context."

I no longer knew what he was talking about, but I did know
that we'd never be able to get within twenty yards of the
Wasserfoygl *sukke*. There'd be cops and ropes and barriers all
over the street.

"You're forgetting one thing," Micah told me. "What time is
it?" My solid gold watch said ten-thirty. "And despite the tragedy,
it's still *Shabbes*, so where's everybody gonna be?" I didn't have
time to answer.

"But if there's no crowd, won't it be even harder to sneak
in?"

He laughed. "Not if we do it properly." And he outlined his
plan.

It was certainly bold enough, but still, "It's *Shabbes*!" I cried.
"You can't do that *Shabbes*."

"Remember, we're talking here about the saving of a life, the
life of *klal yisroel*, the Community of Israel, and the life of your

friend, Micah Mushmelon. Remember what we're fighting for—how could I lead you astray?"

Ten minutes later, clad in one of Micah's roomy capotes, my arms folded tightly over my chest, I began the block and a half walk to the Wasserfoygl residence with Micah Mushmelon at my side.

The streets were deserted. With the exception of a lone police car parked outside the house, there was no indication of anything untoward *chez* Wasserfoygl. Micah found himself a hiding place in the bushes outside the house; before secreting himself, he approached me, ripped the buttons from the capote I was wearing, tore the lapels and punched me in the face with all his strength—twice. The blows knocked me flat, *tukhes* over *tshaynik*, as they say in Jewish. He helped me up, smeared the blood from my nose around my face, and looked appraisingly at his handiwork. "That's gonna be some shiner," he exclaimed with satisfaction. "Ready?" I nodded, biting back the tears. As Micah crawled into the bushes, I turned on the king-size portable radio-tape player I'd been hiding in my capote and which I'd set down on the pavement prior to my beating. Micah had obtained a rap tape from somewhere or other, and it was now playing at full blast.

Within ten seconds, the two policemen detailed to watch the *sukke* came running out from behind the house. I was lying prostrate on the pavement, pointing towards the corner, and screaming in a tear-choked voice, "That way! There they go! Get 'em!"

Ignoring me for the moment, both policemen took off down the street in pursuit of my imaginary assailants. From the corner of my eye, I could see Micah Mushmelon ducking out of the bushes and into the yard. "Keep them talking as long as you can," he had instructed, "and make sure they're always looking across the street."

As one of the cops began trotting back in my direction, I made a show of trying to struggle to my feet. The cop bent over and turned off the tape. He pulled me up by an arm, brushed me off a little and, O my God, began leading me around to the back of the house to wash the blood and dirt off my face. "No!" I barked. "No! It's forbidden to use sprinkler-type water before the official celebration of the Rejoicing at the Drawing of Water." I liked this religion; you could always find a good reason to say no.

"O...K," sang the cop, peering into my face. "Boy, that's gonna be some shiner ... Now, what's your name, son?"

I told him, and where I lived. "I was just walking down the street, when the three of them jumped me ... Right, for no reason; I wouldn't talk to that kind of person even if he talked to me first. One of them had the ghetto-blaster on his shoulder, and the other two were sort of dancing around him, making all kinds of noise."

"Yeah, I was surprised to hear that kind of crap around here," said the cop, who told me to call him Tim.

"It happens once in a while, but usually there's a lot of other people around. Anyway, just as I was about to pass them, one of them, a huge guy, hauled off and smashed me in the face like this," and I gestured with my forearm. "After I fell down, they all started kicking me and jumping on me. Then, I don't know, I guess they saw you coming." I thought of Rabbi Wasserfoygl, of Micah's parents, and began to cry. "Stupid jerks," I sobbed. "If they ever come back here, I'll kill 'em."

The cop tilted my chin up and patted me on the back. "Sure you will. Don't cry, soldier, there was nothing you could do.

Three to one is pretty rough odds." He took a notebook and pen out of his pocket. "Let's see then. They were how old?" I told him about my age, maybe twelve. "Three males, black …"

Meanwhile his partner came back. Tim looked towards him. "Nothing," said the partner. "They just disappeared."

"O…K. We'll get 'em yet." I wasn't quite sure which of us Tim was talking to. "Why don't you put the ghetto-blaster in the black and white while I finish with Sharky here, and then you can call it in … Where were we? Yeah, three males, black …"

"I never said they were black," I interrupted.

"Well, were they?"

"No."

"O…K. Three males, Hispanic?"

"Nope."

"Well, what then?" I could tell he was getting mad.

"I think they were Jewish."

"Jewish? And carrying one of those things on Saturday? C'mon, kid, I been working this beat for three years now."

"I didn't say they were from this neighbourhood, did I?" I tried to sound petulant, a little belligerent even. "I didn't say they were religious. Plenty of Jews aren't, you know."

"All right, all right."

"They called me bad names in Jewish."

"OK already. Three male Caucasians"—I saw Micah Mushmelon wandering towards us down the street. He must have hopped a few fences, the equivalent for him of splitting the Red Sea, and come out of a yard a few houses down. He was flushed, and I could see he was panting. "Age approximately eleven or twelve. How were they dressed?"

"Shraga, that you? What's the matter?" Micah came running up.

"Your friend here's had a little trouble," said Tim, winking to his partner.

"Gosh." Micah was overdoing it a bit. "Is he gonna need a lawyer?"

The cops both laughed. "No, son. Shecky here was the victim."

"*Borukh ha-shem*," said Micah. "Can I take him home?"

*   *   *   *   *

"It's absolutely fantastic," Micah began as soon as we were out of the cops' earshot. "I've never seen anything so fiendishly clever."

"So you've solved it then, the murder?"

"I'd solved it before it ever happened," he bristled. "I had merely to discover how it had been done. And by the way, *mazl tov*. I had no idea you were such an accomplished liar. Why, in the wrong hands ... I shudder to think what might have become of you."

"Thank you. I learned a lot of it from comic books, you know."

"Really?" The possibility seemed never to have occurred to him. "All those stories about talking donkeys really have an effect? I'd never have believed it."

I shrugged my shoulders, turning my palms heavenwards. "So how'd he do it?"

"Ah, yes." Micah was back on track. "It's unbelievable, diabolical in every sense of the word. Of course, the police have found nothing, and will continue to find nothing. I myself was baffled at first. Remember, I needed no clues as to *who* did it, no footprints or any such trifles. My mission was to prove that it was really murder.

"I checked the *sukke* from top to bottom, the walls, the ground, the beds and table. Nothing. I was about to give up when I saw them, hanging from the *skhakh*, tiny and red and deadly; *Acinus florens pharsamticus,* better known to you as *gargerei lilis,* the night-blooming berries of Lilith. A gift from Les Dean, no doubt. These berries are the demonic original of what the *goyim* call the Christmas-you'll-excuse-me-cactus. Like that memorial to the advent of vanity, the a.f.p. flowers but once a year, on the first night of *Sukkes,* releasing an odourless pheromonal vapour which is fatal to any physically mature male, that is to say, any boy or man who already has two pubic hairs." He pronounced the word, poobic.

"This is fantastic!" I exclaimed, thankful for once that no sign of impending manhood had yet appeared anywhere on me. "But how does it work? How does the plant know whether you're a man or a woman?"

"The plant doesn't care; it just does. The hormonal essence is so concentrated that it proves too great a strain on the heart of the victim. He's enveloped in dreams, dirty, filthy sex-dreams which cause him to commit 'the sin against the covenant'."

I'd heard about this in what passed for compulsory sex-education in my school. Apparently, older boys and all men dream about women who look like steamboats, or trains going into tunnels; these dreams make them sort of pee in their sleep. Not only that, but by touching the sign of God's Covenant with Abraham, they can sometimes make themselves do the same thing while awake. I never understood what the big deal was, or why it could only happen after steamboats and trains were invented, except who wants to be a sheet-*pisher* all his life? But the rabbis made it clear that wetting the bed like this was the worst sin you could commit—mass murder, they said—and that if it happened too often you'd end up having nothing but girls after you got married. The only prevention was to work real hard all day so you'd be tired at night, and to say Psalms before you went to bed. It worked, I guess, because I've never wet the bed since I was two or three years old.

Micah, of course, had not stopped talking. "The poison is so virulent, the act of sin so intense, so frequently repeated, that the poor victim's heart finally gives out from the strain. Every death exhibits the same two contradictory features: all the signs of the heart attack which has been suffered, but accompanied by the 'spilling', 'the little death' more usually associated with hanging." Though the chain of reasoning eluded me, I still believed every word he said.

"So," I decided to hazard a guess, "you can tell that they died of one thing, because anybody, a doctor, can tell that it was a heart attack, but there's also, like symptoms of getting hung, even though their necks aren't broken?"

"Absolutely. I'd wager a year's supply of licorice pipes that the late Rabbi Wasserfoygl and his four sons will all be found with traces of ejaculate in their bedclothes. In fact, I'd wager more than that: I took the precaution of examining the sheets on their cots."

I felt even worse than before. It was bad enough for Rabbi Wasserfoygl to get murdered, but to have to leave this world as an adult bed-wetter—Les Dean had killed him twice.

We were approaching the Hipster *bes-medresh*. The whoops and shrieks of thousands of half-drunk, *Shabbes-* and *Sukkes-*happy hasidim could be heard all the way down the block, and Micah didn't want to be disturbed. "Plenty of time later to dance on Les Dean's grave," he muttered. "Right now we've got work to do."

"There's one thing I still don't understand." Shraga-Getsl had seen us safely upstairs. "Determining how they were killed—isn't it like chocolate on matzoh? We already knew who did it, and knowing how doesn't bring us any closer to Les Dean ..."

"The World's Greatest *Apikoyros*," Shraga-Getsl chimed in.

"And without that, I don't see how we're any farther ahead." The sound of the hasidim in the courtyard singing the twelfth century Hymn of Glory to the tune of "Lester Leaps In" penetrated even through the closed windows and doors. Shraga-Getsl began tapping his knee in time to the beat, but stopped at a sharp look from Micah.

"Such progress as you speak of is an eighteenth century concept and should be banished from your mind; look what it did to Les Dean. We are here; The World's Greatest *Apikoyros* is at some unspecified there; we have merely to close the gap. My knowledge of Talmudic botany has already yielded us one valuable clue, namely, the fact that Les Dean must have got the berries from somewhere. They are exceedingly rare, and it would require a certain amount of trouble and planning to obtain them. Secondly, the presence of said berries in the Wasserfoygl *sukke* points to the fact that the oppidian Dean must have volunteered to assist Rabbi Wasserfoygl in the decoration of the mortal hut. The only way in which Les Dean could have accomplished this—remember, he is disguised as a *frum* rabbi—that is, the only valid excuse he could have offered for having the time to decorate somebody else's *sukke* instead of his own would be that his own domicile afforded him no space to put one up. That means—and surely the unfortunate Wasserfoygl would have known this—that Dean is living in an apartment. But, you ask—and rightly so—isn't Brooklyn full of apartment *sukkes*? Isn't everyone—even an apartment dweller—obliged to have his own *sukke?* Absolutely. Everyone but the traveller or sojourner, who must perforce lodge with another. But, you say further, Les Dean lives here, and can hardly be planning to give up his apartment. Correct again. Which tells us that he must have fallen back on the old I'm-a-native-of-the-land-of-Israel ruse; in *mesikhte kesubos,* the tractate on marriage contracts, folio seventy-five, recto, it says, 'And of Zion it is said, this guy and that one were born in her'—Psalm eighty-seven, verse five—which the gemore interprets to mean, one is born there and one hopes to see it, that is, hopes to be there. So that the guy who hopes to be there is subsumed under the rubric of him who was born there, which means that any Jew can legitimately claim birth in the land of Israel. And birth entitles one to citizenship everywhere but Europe. So that Les Dean, The World's Greatest *Apikoyros*—and now, Shraga, you're starting to see what *apikoyros* really means—could present himself to Rabbi Wasserfoygl, to the Community of Israel and to the Holy One Himself as a resident of Israel who is merely here on vacation, as it were. Having done so, he must, however, follow through and actually sleep in the *sukke.*"

"But if he sleeps in the *sukke,* he'll die."

"Precisely. And the weather's so nice these days. And who's exempt from sleeping in the *sukke* when it's nice outside?"

"A sick person, naturally."

"Naturally. What, with a little cold?"

"Mmmm ... in weather like this, you'd have to be pretty sick."

"Yes," said Micah. "Pretty sick—I'm getting hungry, Shraga-Getsl—like in-the-hospital sick."

A Chanukah-*menorah* went on in my head. Shraga-Getsl went out for some food. "There's only one hospital around here that a holy rabbi could go to," I shouted excitedly, "so all we have to do is go over to the Khofets Khaim Pavilion, the He-Who-Desires-Life Hospital, and kill Les Dean!"

"Would God life should be so easy. If we walked in and killed him, we'd end up in reform school, and I've already got my matric … No, Shraga, I have to think."

"Couldn't we just make public what's in *The Black Book on Les Dean?*"

Micah looked at me as if I were a sideshow attraction. "You ever read a Yiddish paper? Take away the slander and accusations, you wouldn't even have the ads left. And who gets denounced most of all? *Nu?*"

"The Lubavitcher Rebbe … And the Satmarer Rebbe."

"And who are the biggest rebbes in America?"

I held up my hand. "*Sapienti sat,* Micah."

Shraga-Getsl re-entered the room with a giant tray of shmaltz herring, *cholent, kugel,* smoked salmon and *knoblwurst*. Micah no sooner looked at it than he began to speak. "I think I've got an idea, but first tell me, Potasznik. Knowing what you now know, why do you think Les Dean wanted you out of Oykrei Horim?"

As the *cholent* flowed into Micah's mouth, I considered the question. I'd never had any idea why Les Dean had thrown me out, why he'd trumped up the charges against me. But I could see now that Les Dean never did anything for its own sake, there was always an ulterior motive. Yet even two minutes later, when Micah had finished his pudding and both kinds of fish, I was still unable to come up with a single transgression. I shrugged my shoulders.

"You didn't do anything wrong?" Micah asked. I shook my head. "Nothing except exist!" he cried. "Tell me, did Les Dean always know who you were—by name, I mean?"

I thought another moment. My head was beginning to hurt; the fumes from the *knoblwurst* were making me dizzy. "I don't think so. There was an awful lot of us, and I wasn't a troop leader or anything like that. I wasn't too famous, if that's what you mean."

"Just a face in the crowd, huh? And you were kicked out last summer. And what do all the Oykrei Horim do in the summer?"

"Uproot mountains in the mountains." I repeated the slogan of the group's summer camp and wiped away a tear, half wurst and half regret.

"And in order to do so, to organize the trip, contact the parents, make reservations, somebody has to go through the list of members, no?" It seemed to make sense. "And it's obvious that that someone was Les Dean. During their first year, of course, they couldn't have organized a camp, but late last spring, when he reached your name—remember how I told you that you were very special, Shraga? Well, it's probably the only thing in the world on which Les Dean and I agree. When he came to your name, a bell must have sounded in his head like for a five-alarm fire." I was more bewildered than flattered, nice as it was to be special. "You know anything about *gematria?*" Micah asked.

"A little," I told him. "It's when you take the Hebrew letters as numbers—like *aleph* is one, *beys* is two and so on—and figure out what number a word comes out to. And then, if you want, you can substitute words that have the same numerical value for each other. Like when it says in the Shma that God is one—you know already that you have to love God, because the word for one, *ekhod*, is aleph, which is one; *khes*, which is eight; and *dalet*, which is four—thirteen. And the word for love, *ahavah*, also adds up to thirteen. So you know that by saying that God is one that you also have to love Him, like the next word in the prayer tells you, 'And you must love the Lord.' It also lets you know that once you're thirteen, bar-mitzvah, you've gotta love Him by doing His *mitsves*."

"That's very good, Shraga." He sounded so grown-up. "You really do understand it. Now, how were you registered in Oykrei Horim?"

"Just as Shraga Potasznik. Like I told Shraga-Getsl, I never use my middle name."

"I don't blame you … But think. Shraga equals five hundred and four, the same as … *Nu*, any idea?" I was stumped. "The same as Les Dean, may his name be blotted out! And Potasznik is the same as the phrase *glaykht isso din*, 'equals there is a judgment'. For what does Les Dean's name mean?"

"There is no judgment."

"And what does Shraga Potasznik mean? That Shraga, that your very existence is equal to the proof that there is a judgment—and hence a judge. Don't you see, Shraga? Every other Shraga in the Oykrei Horim must have used his middle name; but you, you … I am Les Dean's enemy, but you are his negation. You can be substituted for him, you can cancel him out; instead of saying, '*Les Dean, Les Dayan,* there is no judgment and there is no judge,' you can say, '*Shraga, Shraga,* Light, Light,' and blow the evil force-husks off the map of creation. So long as you remained in Oykrei Horim, Les Dean was stymied, powerless to act. He had to be rid of you in order to be able to proceed with his plans. And to think, were it not that Shraga-Getsl here gets advance copies of *Khamoro Kadisho* comics, I might never have found you."

"So it really was no accident, outside the comic shop?"

"I'd been waiting there all day."

"And I really am somebody special? It wasn't just a line?"

"The power of your name is the mainstay of our hopes."

"And you were really looking for me ever since you left the yeshiva in heaven?"

"Without let or surcease."

"Then why didn't you look in the phone book?" I screamed. "It was there all the time."

Shraga-Getsl's mouth dropped open. "By Rachel thy naked daughter, I've never heard such *khutspe* in my life. Want me to work him over, Rebbe?"

Micah Mushmelon laughed and made with his hand. *"Shabbes,"* he said. "Every dog has his day."

I guess it was the idea of being really special for the first time in my life—I was sort of drunk on it. "I'm sorry, Micah. It must have been the *knoblwurst.*"

Micah looked at it quizzically, popped it into his mouth. "Tastes OK to me," he said. "I already explained it to you: in heaven you had no name. It's one of God's loving kindnesses that my old best friend is also my secret weapon in the struggle against Les Dean." He paused for a moment to swallow the *knoblwurst.* "Now, let's get back to my plan. Now that you know who you are, Potasznik, now that the concept of the naked Shraga has been made clear, we can swing into action. Rabbi Wasserfoygl and his poor sons will not be buried until Monday; tomorrow night, however, was to have been the giant Oykrei Horim rally, which will undoubtedly be transformed into a memorial tribute to the organization's founder—led, naturally, by Les Dean. He will move heaven and earth with his plaint, carrying the innocents off on a wave of rhetoric, until he reaches his climax: the transformation of Oykrei Horim, a kosher *mitsve* brigade, into The Elisha ben Avuyah Fan Club."

The words made me shudder. "We have to stop him before it's too late. We have to expose Les ..." I slapped myself on the forehead. "But who's gonna believe us?" I asked in despair. "Les Dean is a grown-up rabbi. Who's going to take the word of a couple of *pishers* like us?"

"Nobody, Shraga. That's why we have to enlist some outside help. Shraga-Getsl, bring me The Girls."

*   *   *   *   *

To Micah Mushmelon they were always The Girls; to the rest of the neighbourhood they were *the* girls, the only girls, the distilled essence of Female. Seven and eight year old boys, snot-noses with grass-stains on their *tsitsis* who wouldn't ask a *girl* for matzoh at the seder, buckled and swooned at the sight of them. Grown men were known to follow them around, and more than one shop-keeper and rabbi had stumbled with his hands while talking to them. Even Micah Mushmelon, who had written a responsum stating that "the great thing about this religion is that nobody can make you play with girls," even Micah Mushmelon would dust off his *dashikl* if he knew they were coming and set it straight upon his head.

They came by it naturally, The Girls, by way of their mother. A converted Follies girl from Paris who had married a Hipster hasid, Dina de Malchusa (she used her maiden name for public appearances) made a fine living giving women's lectures and entertainment programs around town: "Slay Him with *Tsnies*,"

"No Pockets in a *Mikve*"—that sort of thing. Yeah, they came by it honestly, The Girls did; twelve years old, and when they walked down the street there was nothing but calf and thigh and crinkles in their blouse that had nothing to do with the laundry.

Froyke Buvv, the Hipster hasid and Sorbonne Ph.D. who converted and then married Mademoiselle de Malchusa, was pitied like a charity case. He alone couldn't drool over The Girls. It would have been unseemly.

For whatever It is, his daughters, Tess and Tisha, had it—and to spare. And Micah Mushmelon, as Hipster Rebbe Designate, had them. "It's only a question of which one I'll marry," he used to say. He'd even embarked on a project to try and repeal the prohibition of polygamy, until Shraga-Getsl pointed out that it wouldn't make any difference: when it came to what counted, no one could tell them apart. True, they both dressed in black from head to toe, both their heads were crowned with thick black hair falling to their backsides; it was true that they were identical twins. But this isn't what Shraga-Getsl meant. No, in the middle of maybe hundreds of Talmud Torahs, yeshivas, *bes-medreshes* and secretarial colleges, Tess and Tisha Buvv had established their own clandestine academy, *Neshikoys Pihu*, The Kisses of His Mouth, tuition a dollar a minute, with a fifteen minute class limit, students to sit on their hands.

The charity boxes at school had been covered with cobwebs since the smooch academy had opened. A new term began with each of their mother's lectures; since they lived in an apartment building, the coming and going of the boys could scarcely be noticed. The climactic lesson, the one that had given rise to the view that the two girls were indistinguishable, consisted of one long kiss, starting with one of the girls and culminating with the other: the student was forbidden to break rhythm or stride, had to make the transition as smoothly as possible, and his eyes had to be closed at all times. No one had ever noticed the switch.

The existence of Neshikoys Pihu was known to no grown-up, save perhaps Shraga-Getsl; even sucks who disapproved kept their mouths shut, terrified of the vengeance that was certain to come. Half the boys in Oykrei Horim were wandering around with chapped lips; the other half were saving their pennies.

Me, I was happy with the *Times* crossword and my comic collection, but on those sleepless nights when I pretended to be marooned on a desert island, *they* were always there, usually in girl-cut Tarzan suits.

Can you blame me, then, for yelling out, "The Torah Sluts?" when Micah sent Shraga-Getsl after them? That's how they were called by the older guys, and I was pretty shocked when Micah removed his *dashikl*, revealing his velvet yarmulke and hairless pate for the first time since I'd met him, and began beating me over the head with it, *Shabbes* or no *Shabbes*. "I warned you already, never say that again!" he hollered, punctuating each word with a fresh blow. "Don't even try and think it. These Girls have sacrificed their time, their lips, their mother's sofa, all so that Jewish boys might pant to be married and study kabbala, and you have the nerve to insult them? You should be ashamed in your farthest neck. Under whose auspices do you think Neshikoys Pihu operates? Have you forgotten that they are the daughters of Hipst?"

I'd thought that their activities smacked more of Les Dean than of the Mushmelon holiness.

"Don't be an idiot," he said. "These are not Italian mice, and the lesson you're about to get from them is the culmination, the end and justification, of their entire academic career. After today, God willing, they'll go into voluntary retirement."

As Shraga-Getsl led them in, I remarked on how religious their black tights made them look.

"We're like beatniks," they said together, snapping their fingers.

Beatniks, I thought. Beatniks went out with my parents' childhood.

"Like Allen Ginsberg?" I asked.

They snapped assent.

"I think you Girls should know," Micah announced, "that Shraga here was intended to be Allen Ginsberg's son, until a cruel fate and the anger of a Pharisee deflected his soul from its true course."

Within seconds they were on top of me—Micah told me later that I'd even gone through the graduate course and passed *cum laude.* When I woke up, my covenant was like a telephone pole, but my pants, thank God, were dry.

Shraga-Getsl brought me no food this time. "He's gone out," said Micah, "On urgent business. Just sit tight and don't ask any questions. It's now …"

He looked at me and I checked my watch. "Eleven forty-seven."

"Good. Let us join my flock. At four o'clock I want you to go to the hospital and visit Les Dean."

"Maybe I should slit my throat?" Micah was beginning to have an influence on me. "Won't that put him on guard?"

"He'll think you're nursing a grudge. Remember, he's as powerless as a new-born babe in your presence. Just stand there and smile and say your name. Don't say anything else. Just repeat your name. If you want, you can cackle."

I spent most of the afternoon in the bathroom, practising my mad scientist laugh. I think it's permitted on *Shabbes.*

VII

POISED BETWEEN TERROR AND ANTICIPATION, I hurried the six blocks to the Khofets Khaim Pavilion through capote-darkened streets. Whatever Les Dean might try and do to me, I realized that he'd attribute the whole thing to my expulsion from Oykrei Horim. He had no way of knowing that Mushmelon had made contact, he could never suspect that I now knew of my powers. I'd often wondered how *meshiekh* could wander the earth without knowing who he was until the Holy One chose to reveal him to himself, but here I was, a little *meshiekh*, the potential saviour of *yidishkayt* as we know it, and I'd had no inkling of the fact until five hours before. Truth, I decided, was stranger than fiction.

As I approached the hospital, I was seized with horror. A crowd was milling about the grounds, four or five thousand people probably, all of them waving up at a window, shouting good wishes for a speedy recovery while standing in a huge s-shaped line and waiting to be admitted. "So fast?" I wondered. Had Les Dean mobilized the adults while we were worrying about the kids?

"Vus tit zakh du?" I asked the nearest Jew. "What's happening here?"

"The Skiffler Gaon." He gestured toward a window on the top floor. "Rushed him in about noon. The gout again."

The Skiffler was said to have gone to *kheyder* with the Warner Brothers, and the Jew must have thought I was thanking God that gout was all it was. At the information desk, I discovered that Les Dean and the Gaon were sharing a room. According to the records, Rabbi Dean was in for water on his hip. I wondered who had injected him.

Breaking through the mob lined up to bless the Skiffler's toe and be blessed by him in turn would be like throwing a tackle at the Statue of Liberty. Designed for the medical and religious comfort of Moses Maimonides, the Khofets Khaim Pavilion was laid out in unusual fashion. A mere three storeys high, the building covered at least an acre of ground; the low height made it possible for people to come and visit on the Sabbath without even having to think about an elevator. Indeed, there were no *stairs* in the public parts of the hospital, out of consideration for the advanced age of many of the visitors and patients. Rather, curving ramps led from one level to another, with large rest-stop landings at the second floor. There were about half a dozen of these ramps scattered at equal distances along the length of the building, so that what you had, in effect, was an airport terminal devoted solely to waiting. It was said to have been named for the Khofets Khaim, not only because of his universal prestige in the religious world—he was accepted by every faction—or the happy accident of his name, but also to commemorate his famous lack of height.

Every ramp was packed solid with waiting people, most of them hasidim, all of them engaged in normative hasidic recreation—intramural pushing. Shoving and yelling and grunting, they swayed backwards and forwards, tilting dangerously along the inclines of the ramps. You couldn't have got a drinking straw through. I considered what Micah Mushmelon would have done, but lacked self-confidence and bulk, not to mention Shraga-Getsl. I had to think for myself. Setting a small fire could prove dangerous: it being *Shabbes*, I'd have been stoned to death as soon as I struck a match. I wouldn't have known where to find a live pig even if I'd been in the habit of carrying money *Shabbes*, and in this neighbourhood, I couldn't even get a ham sandwich to throw. I was wandering around the ground floor, thinking how strange it was that a saint like the Skiffler Gaon should end up in the same room with a monster like Les Dean, when I noticed a section of the crowd cleaving open like the rock at Meribah. I gave a look, and saw the trademark fuschia *bekeshe* of the Gryfter Rov making its way through the throng, obviously on the way to see the Skiffler. The presence of the famous scholar gave me the inspiration I needed.

I waited five minutes or so, long enough for the Gryfter to get up to room 364—seven times *kelev*, dog, in *gematria*—then walked twenty feet outside, dishevelled myself, and came running in, one hand on my cap, the other clutching my heart, as if I'd just run a marathon at the pace of a dash. *"Ratevet, yidn, ratevet!"* I shouted frantically. "Help! Help! The big Popielnitshker *bes-medresh*, it's on fire! Save the Torah scrolls! The Rebbe's inside!"

I leapt away from the door and thanked God that all hasidic children look the same from a distance. The Rebbe of Popielnitshke was only the second biggest in town in terms of number of followers, but he had strong political ambitions and was popular as hell. He never attacked anybody. He was also the Skiffler Gaon's best friend.

I'd spent my life in this world; I knew that no one would so much as glance at a window to see if there was any smoke. Within sixty seconds at most, there were maybe two dozen people wandering around the second floor of the hospital, and the grounds outside were empty. I was feeling pretty important; not even bar-mitzvah, and I'd already started a major rumour. I would have whistled as I went up the ramp, only it was *Shabbes* and whistling is anyway only for *goyim*—let them deal with the *sheydim*.

Room 364 was three to the right from the top of the ramp; I could already hear a familiar voice coming out of it. I walked in. Les Dean was in the bed closest to the door. There were eighteen or twenty hasidim crowded round the Skiffler's bed, and flanking Les Dean's like a guard of honour, one on either side, stood my mother and father. "Shraga!" they both yelled delightedly. Les Dean stared in silence. The Skiffler moved a hasid out of the way and took a look. The Gryfter was nowhere to be seen. *"Hob nish' ka moyre, yingele. Kim-zhe aher,"* he said with a smile and a wink. "Don't be afraid, kid. Come on over." I shook my head and pointed to Les Dean. *"Shaygets,"* said the Gaon ambiguously, and returned to his hasidim.

"What a wonderful surprise!" my mother said. "O my God, what happened to your eye? What have those awful Hipsters done to you? I knew we should never have let you go."

Les Dean sat bolt upright; I didn't know what to do, so I just stood there. He might not connect me with Micah—lots of people went to watch the Hipsters—he couldn't run off without blowing his cover, and he could do no evil in my presence. Only I couldn't stay there forever.

"That's quite a shiner, son," said my father. "Let's have a look."

"My name is Shraga Potasznik," I said, as my father bent over my face, poking me where it hurt the most.

"Loser"—the Polish pronunciation of Elazar—"it's affected his mind. We'd better check him in." My mother looked ready to faint.

"Nonsense. He's just playing soldier, aren't you, son?"

"Yeah, that's right. Name, rank and serial number."

"You see? Oykrei Horim's making a man of him."

"Shraga Potasznik!" I yelled, saluting.

"I think he'll be all right."

"Yeah. I only tripped on a *sukke*," I said, trying to talk out of the corner of my mouth. "Shraga Potasznik." I was embarrassed even in front of Les Dean.

"All right, then," said my mother, continuing from where she'd left off; talking on three telephones at once had given her certain skills. "We came up to see the Skiffler Gaon and ask him to give you a blessing for success in your new school and that you should find a good match ..."

"Well, of course, it wasn't really we," my father chimed in. "True, it was a mutual decision to give the Gaon your new issue of *Khamoro Kadisho*"—I was sure that the Skiffler, whose works were so profound as to be banned to anyone under forty, appreciated the gesture—"but as you know, son, us males past barmitzvah can't really be in the company of strange women. Now, although the presence of so many other men in the room, plus the presence of *her* man"—my mother giggled—"would make it all right for most anybody, the Skiffler Gaon is so holy that we didn't want to risk offending him." Or getting Mama killed, I thought. "So I arrived at an expedient. Yes, the government of this great country doesn't value the services of Loser Potasznik for nothing."

"Dad, you sort mail," I said.

My mother gave me a dirty look.

My father simply cleared his throat and went on as if nothing had happened. "Yes, I arrived at an expedient. I had your mother wait outside the room while I asked whether she might come in. And as we came in, who do you think I saw? Your old friend, Rabbi Dean. He's been wondering why you haven't been to any meetings lately"—The World's Greatest *Apikoyros*, indeed! He'd figured I'd be too ashamed to tell my parents, and he was right. No wonder my father thought that Oykrei Horim had made a man of me—"and he hoped, in light of the terrible tragedy, the calamity, the horror unheard of in all the years of creation, woe to the generation that has seen its leaders thus plucked from its midst, that you'd be coming back to Oykrei Horim now."

Les Dean was staring at me with an evil sneer on his face. So it's like this, is it? I thought. He knows that I know—my mother had made sure of that—perhaps not how much, but he knows that I know something.

"Yes, Shraga," said my mother, "Why didn't you tell us that you quit?"

Quit? That was more than I could take. Here they were, people who thought they were my parents—worse, whom everybody else thought were my parents—defending Les Dean to my face, taking his lying word that everything was all my fault.

"Yeah," said my father, drawing the sleeve of his capote over the tip of his nose. "I never thought I'd live to see the day when a son of mine would have the *khutspe*, the unmitigated gall, to turn his back on a rabbinic figure of the stature of Rabbi Dean."

Les Dean was smiling now. Powerless as my presence had rendered him, he could see that we were doing his work for him.

"Number one," I started, "I'm not your son." My parents looked from one to the other, startled. "I never was your son and I never will be. I was given to you as a punishment—don't interrupt—because of a prank I pulled in heaven. I am not your son," I repeated. "I am the *fils manqué* of Allen Ginsberg, the son he never had. I am a beatnik ben beatnik, a poet ben poet, and because of you and your … your lectures and *yortsayts* and tiny brains, because I had the bad luck to hit Shammai instead of Hillel, Allen Ginsberg has become a Buddhist"—at this, the entire room, including the Skiffler and all his visitors, yelled out a *rakhmone litslan*—"*and* I have had to spend my life in a home for retarded adults." I heard the Skiffler Gaon laughing.

"Number two, I never quit Oykrei Horim. Rabbi Dean"—I didn't want to tip my hand completely—"kicked me out. Made up charges and threw me out. He said that you," I pointed to my mother, "were a racial Litvak with a driver's licence." My mother turned white.

"Is any of this true?" My father addressed himself to Les Dean in what was supposed to be a stern tone of voice, but only managed to sound like a kid trying to imitate an adult.

"Mr. Potasznik, I haven't the slightest idea what the boy is talking about. I'm hardly the right person to ask about his parentage."

My father mulled this over. "You're right," he said. "Shraga, telling lies is not a good character trait. The Post Office demands honesty. Also, it isn't the Jewish way. Start off with little fibs, next thing you know, you'll be Pope."

"Idiot, *bulvan*, Christmas seal! Ask him about Oykrei Horim! Find out why he kicked me out."

"I don't know that he did," my father said, turning and beginning to head in my direction. "And if this is any indication of the way you behave, Rabbi Dean was entirely justified."

"Rabbi Dean, Rabbi Dean as you call him, is never justified."
I used the technical term for justified, and the whole room
turned to look at me. The Skiffler's head was sticking out from
between the legs of two of his comforters. "Rabbi Dean is Les
Dean, The World's Greatest *Apikoyros* and the Manischewitz
of Crime! He killed Micah Mushmelon's parents"—a little bell
went off in my head. I'd done it now. Well, what the hell: *az men
est khazer, zol rinnen fun bord,* if you eat pig, lick your lips—"He
killed his grandfather! He killed Rabbi Wasserfoygel and his
four sons!" I no longer noticed what my parents were thinking.
"He kicked me out of Oykrei Horim because as long as I'm
around, his evil cannot operate," and I explained to them what
Micah Mushmelon had explained to me. The Skiffler Gaon was
clapping his hands together like a baby in a carseat. "You don't
believe me? Watch! Watch this! Shraga Potasznik, Shraga
Potasznik!" I was screaming directly into Les Dean's face.
"Shraga Potasznik is not Les Dean! Shraga Potasznik means that
God is One!" Dean lay immobile. "Shraga in the *mikve*, Les Dean
in der erd, Shraga in the *mikve,* Les Dean *in der erd.*" He glared at
me with hatred. *"Mikve yisroel adoyshem,* God is our hope and
our ritual bath. You're finished, Les, all washed up ... Washed
up, that was a good one.

> *Mikve yisroel,*
> *Mikve* mouse,
> *Mikve* mckinley,
> Les Dean, *raus!"*

He was pale, unmoving.
"You see," I turned to the crowd. "He can do no evil when
I'm around. And since all his ways are twisted, he can't even

move or do anything. When it comes to Les Dean," I added proudly, "I'm Kryptonite."

But I'd stopped saying my name, and simple function was returning to the miscreant. I could hear him humming "*Guantanamera*." "Shraga Potasznik!" I yelled six or eight times. To tell the truth, I wasn't so happy as I looked. Whatever beans my mother had left, I'd spilled but good, and I didn't know how to get out. Sure, I could walk out the door, but I couldn't have given Les Dean a clearer idea of what I was doing if I'd invited him over to the Hipster *bes-medresh*. I just stood there saying my name, which was beginning to sound pretty stupid.

"You there, ex-father." I was so desperate I no longer knew what to do. "Go downstairs and ask for the telephone ... Don't look so shocked, this is *pikuakh nefesh*. Get the number of the Hipster *Shabbes*-emergency red-phone and ..."

"No need, Shraga." It was Micah Mushmelon himself, accompanied by Shraga-Getsl and the Buvv twins. "We've been outside all the time. Just wanted to see how you'd handle your maiden assignment, and I must say, you've come through with flying colours. Or almost."

At the sight of Micah Mushmelon, Les Dean began to sputter and squirm. "Mushmelon!" he hissed. "I should have taken care of you when I had the chance."

"There is no chance, Les Dean, only divine providence," said Micah Mushmelon. "Isn't that right, Itche?"

"You said it, Micah," said, of all people, the Skiffler Gaon.

I looked at Micah. "We go way back, the Skiffler and me. He came in here as a safety net, in case some catastrophe befell me and you choked at the last minute. Which you—Shraga Potasznik!" he screamed, pointing at me. The bedclothes ceased their rustle. "Which you did. And now, Itche, so that you shouldn't have had to ruin your *Shabbes* for nothing, give him the word."

"Shraga," said the Skiffler Gaon, "Kiss Les Dean," I looked at him in shock. "You heard me, kiss him."

I crept over to the bed, whispering my name all the while as a precaution, and gave The World's Greatest *Apikoyros* a peck on the cheek.

"Not like that, you, you …"

"Precocious heterosexual," said Tisha Buvv, licking her lips.

"Yeah," added Micah. "Like you did with The Girls. Flat on the mouth … A little tongue, a little tongue," he cried as I put my lips to Les Dean's mouth. At the mention of delicatessen, my quasi-father began to pace. "More tongue. That's it. Pretend he's Tess, pretend he's Tisha."

"C'mon, Shraga." It was the twins. "Go for the record." Shraga-Getsl began to pinch Les Dean.

I thrust my tongue into his open mouth and half-way down his throat and held on for dear life. I'd never have believed I could hold my breath for so long. My lungs were beginning to ache, I could see spots before my eyes. "How long before I get the bends?" I wondered.

Everything was getting black. I was going down, down, into a deep, relaxing pool. I could see myself speaking with the Holy Talking Donkey, whose voice was that of Micah Mushmelon. "Feed my sheep," he was saying. I had no idea what he meant. The donkey was gone, my parents were there. Allen Ginsberg appeared and said, "Shakti." My mother said, *"Shatkhn."* Ginsberg was about to do something, when a thousand coloured lights went off in my head, and I was knocked over by a wave of sound and a rush of air. It was like somebody had stuck a big needle into the huge Christmas-present-idol balloon that they have in the Macy's parade. Next thing I knew, Micah and Shraga-Getsl were helping me up from the floor—again. There was a funny smell in the room, and my clothes were covered with something that looked like barf.

"Success!" said Micah Mushmelon, pointing to the sodden but empty bed. *"Mazl tov, Shraga, yasher koyekh."* The whole room echoed his salute. Micah looked me up and down just as he had on Wednesday outside the comic book store. "C'mon, we'll go to the *mikve.*"

The Buvv twins squealed and the five of us walked out. "Later, Itche," Micah waved to the Skiffler.

VIII

"BUT WHAT HAPPENED TO THE GRYFTER ROV?" I asked later. We were reclining in the private *sukke*, nibbling from bunches of grapes held over our mouths by the Buvvs. Their dainty hands hung over a makeshift *mekhitse*; Shraga-Getsl had stood the table on end.

"There was no Gryfter Rov," said Micah. "It was Shraga-Getsl. We wanted to be there when you needed us. Shraga-G. just kept his face down. After all, anybody who sees a fuschia *beskeshe* with rhinestone-studded white stockings just thinks Gryfter and doesn't even look."

"And how'd the Skiffler Gaon just happen to be there?"

"Shraga-Getsl went for him while you were with The Girls. The Gaon is a profound mystic; he's known about Les Dean for years, and he really does have terrible gout."

"And sending me alone like that?"

He shrugged. "We had no choice."

"And is Les Dean really dead?"

"Yes and no." Micah reached up and shoved the whole bunch of grapes into his mouth at once. "The evil husks of which he is composed have been scattered, but that is not to say that they won't re-form some time in the future. No, Les Dean can't be killed for good until the coming of *meshiekh tsidkeynu*, the Messiah of our righteousness, when the husks will be returned to their proper place and even Les Dean himself, The World's Greatest *Apikoyros* and Manischewitz of Crime, will become *kuloy zakay*, entirely worthy."

I let this sink in for a minute or two, then asked, "What will cause the husks to re-form?"

"It could be almost anything," Micah said. "The wind, evil deeds, folk music—it's impossible to tell. It takes at least ninety days, though. And after that … don't worry, we'll know."

I liked that we. Micah had already arranged to convene a *bezdin*, a rabbinical court, to appoint me a ward of the lavishly stationeryed Shoymer Pesoyim orphans' home. My father was a *bor*—that's Hebrew for boor—and it says that a boor isn't afraid of sin. How then could I receive a proper upbringing in such a home? For once, my father's reputation was going to do me some good.

Meanwhile, a group of hasidim had appeared at the entrance to our *sukke*. "Re-be, Shra-ga, Re-be, Shra-ga," they were chanting. They bore us out on their shoulders.

Tess and Tisha waved shyly from behind the table. "Hurry back, Shraga," they cooed. "We're gonna give you a Ph.D."

GLOSSARY

Adoyn Oylom—Eternal Lord, a well-known hymn
Aliye—a calling up to the Torah in the synagogue
Amerike gonif—"Rapscallion America," an exclamation of astonishment
Apikorses—heresy
Apikoyros—heretic
Arzei Levonoyn—cedars of Lebanon

Bekeshe—hasidic festive smoking jacket
Bes-medresh—study house, small synagogue
Bokher—see *yeshiva*
Borukh ha-Shem—Blessed be God
Bris—circumcision
Bulvan—moron

Capote—caftan, long black coat worn by hasidim
Cholent—a bean stew eaten on Sabbath

Daven(ing)—pray(ing)
Dus hot mir gefelt—Just what I needed

Erev—eve of

Frum—pious

Gaon—genius
Gemore—Talmud
Gleikhgiltik—indifferent
Goyisher kop—gentile head

In gantsn—completely

Kashrus—kosherness
Khale, take—"taking dough," a "women's" commandment
Kheyder—elementary Hebrew school
Kugel—a savoury pudding

Lulav—a palm branch used on *Sukkes*

Mayim Khayim—Living Water, a brand of kosher soft drink
Mekhitse—divider between the sexes
Mikve—ritual bath
Minkhe—afternoon service
Minyan—quorum of ten adult males for prayer
Mitsve—positive commandment, good deed

Nebekh—an exclamation of pity

Payes—sidelocks

Rakhmone litslan—God save us
Rashi—classical commentator on Bible and Talmud

Shatkhn—marriage broker
Shaygets—goy (male)
Shepping nakhes—drawing pleasure
Sheydim—demons
Shikker iz a goy—"A gentile is drunk," a Yiddish folksong
Shma—Comfession of faith (Deut. 6:4,ff.)
Shokling—shaking, especially in prayer and study
Skhakh—branched roof of a *sukke*

Talmud Torah—Hebrew school
Tanna—mishnaic sage
Tefillin—phylacteries
Treyf—unkosher, unclean
Tsaddik—righteous man, saint
Tsitsis—fringed (under)garment
Tsnies—modesty

Yasher koyekh—Well done, good work
Yeshiva bokher—yeshiva boy
Yikhes—pedigree
Yortsayt—anniversary of death

Zeyde—grandfather

MEMBER OF SCABRINI GROUP

Québec, Canada
2007